THE SECOND ARMADA GHOST BOOK

Charlene McCrory
Primary 7 S

The Second Armada Ghost Book

Edited by

CHRISTINE BERNARD

ILLUSTRATED BY
GINO D'ACHILLE

Armada

The Second Armada Ghost Book was first
published in the U.K. in 1968 by May Fair
Books Ltd, 14 St. James's Place, London,
S.W.1, and was printed in Great Britain by
Love & Malcomson Ltd, Brighton Road,
Redhill, Surrey.

CONTENTS

INTRODUCTION

WE HAVE had a lot of letters from Armada readers about our First Ghost Book—all, I am happy to say, enthusiastic, many of them begging for more. So more is what this book consists of. Some of these stories are from the same authors, others from new and different writers, quite unlike those that appeared in the first collection.

I have given pride of place to Sorche Nic Leodhas' *Ghost who didn't want to be a Ghost*. He has something in common with *The Inexperienced Ghost* who appeared in the first Armada Ghost Book. Both are odd men out, unsuited to their profession, both stories are funny and both have neat twists to their tails—though I feel that this, younger ghost was the luckier in having a fine 'chief' to solve his problems so generously!

Sometimes, even in very good stories, you can't, however hard you try, quite believe in the plot. One reason I have included two of William Croft Dickinson's tales is that you feel sure the events related actually happened. He writes about quite ordinary things like walls and maps and cars; but by the time he has finished with them they have become a great deal *less* ordinary, so that you find yourself looking at workaday objects with new eyes.

The Isle of Man has always been regarded as a romantic and mysterious place and is said to be one of the oldest and most famous centres of witchcraft and the occult. *Fiddler, Play Fast, Play Faster* has all the haunting qualities I have come to associate with this beautiful island. It is a tale 'so old it has grown ragged with the telling so that only a scrap here and there is left' . . . which in itself is an excellent summing up of all legends.

Nothing particularly alarming happens in *The Magic Shop*, yet H. G. Wells' story leaves one strangely uncomfortable, rather put out. Is the shopman a good man or a bad one? If good, what was the little red devil doing in the shop? If bad, why was he so generous to Gyp . . .? *The Flowering of the Strange Orchid* is probably one of the same author's best-known stories. The idea of plants rebelling against their boring existence and taking an active hand in their fate is rather a pleasing one (At school in Botany Classes the insect-eating Sundew flower was far and away *my* favourite); and though such upstarts have to be put in their place it is nice to hear of one rebelling occasionally!

My own favourite in this collection is *Mr. Fox*. I admit this rather guiltily as it can't honestly be called a ghost story—and it is the only one here that has no author. It is an old, old, English folk story and the name of the author has long since been lost. It was old in Shakespeare's time, for in his play, *Much Ado About Nothing*, one of the characters, Benedick, says (using the same words exactly), 'Like the old tale my lord: "It is not so, nor t'was not so, but indeed, God forbid it should be so." ' It has also what I consider to be one of the nicest opening sentences ever written: 'Lady Mary was young, and Lady Mary was fair. She had two brothers and more admirers than she could count. . . ."

And last but not least, *The Ugly-Wuglies*. I very much hope you will enjoy this strange account by Edith Nesbit. Her famous novels, *Five Children and It*, *The Railway Children*, *The House of Arden* and many others (some of which you will have seen dramatised on television), gripped and held me as no other stories ever did. The fact that her children lived in Edwardian times, added to, rather than lessened the charm they had for me. Within a few pages the gas lamps, carriages, frilly dresses and knickerbocker suits became familiar and 'ordinary'. . . . Her very real children have fantastic, *believable* adventures, while her horrors are always that much more horrific, her fears more fearful. The Ugly-Wuglies with their backs to the wall and their 'stick-boned arms stretched out angrily towards the world' are indelibly printed in my mind.

One thing these writers all have in common is a free-flowing imagination which they use to their full bent. And I hope that some of their stories will stir *your* imagination and lead you to explore the world of the mind and all its pleasures, as well as the more tangible one around us.

CRISTINE BERNARD

THE GHOST THAT DIDN'T WANT TO BE A GHOST

By Sorche Nic Leodhas

THERE USED to be a Glasgow man who was in the way of keeping a house for travellers beyond the town on the Great Western Road. He was a grand one for telling tales of ghosts and eerie happenings, and could keep at it for hours at a stretch, or at any rate as long as he had breath enough left to tell them with. He made a point of never telling a story unless he could swear to it that it was the solemn truth. He'd tell the place and date it happened and the name of the man or woman it happened to so that anyone could go and prove it for himself. He had a great liking for one story and told it often, about a ghost that didn't want to be a ghost. He said he got the story from the ghost of the old chief in the story. The old ghost used to stop in to keep him company now and then when the Glasgow man was all alone in his place. The Glasgow man could take you into the town and show you the very house where it happened, because he knew the lad in the tale when he himself was a lad.

The way it happened was that there was a clan of

ghosts under an old Highland chief—one of the Mac-Donalds, no doubt. At any rate he was a fine old ghost and when he was a living, breathing man he had a great reputation for keeping all the clansmen and tenants under him well in hand and making them like it into the bargain. When he got over into the spirit world he used the same methods. They put a lot of ghosts under him there for him to be chief of, and it worked very well. In no time at all he had them taking their condition out-of-life as something that couldn't be helped and making the best of it. He even got them to feeling a certain pride and satisfaction in being ghosts and doing all they could to make a success of their work.

Everything was going along fine and easy, with every ghost of them busy and happy and the old chief proud of them all, when a new young ghost was sent over to take his place among them. It didn't take the ghosts of the old chief's clan long to find out that he was not one of their kind at all.

The fellow was always moping about in corners. He refused to find a place of his own to haunt, and when they went to the trouble of finding one for him, he didn't like it at all. You never met such a ghost for complaining. There was naught in the place that he couldn't find something wrong with. He said the house he was haunting in was too dark and damp and dismal, and it made him ache all over. He said he didn't care for the colour of his shroud, it being such a dirty shade of grey. He said that he didn't see why he should bother to go out haunting when there was such a lot of them that seemed to enjoy doing it while

10

as for himself he found no pleasure in it at all. Then there were those chains they all had to carry around and clank. They were far too heavy, he told them. Anyway, why fash themselves with chains? Och, 'twas all a pack o' nonsense!

They tried to reason with him but it did no manner of good. He said he'd not asked anyone to let him be a ghost and he'd not be pretending he liked to be one. He got very rude about it and told them to go on about their ghosting and just leave him be.

So he just went along moping and complaining and wandering about aimlessly, getting into the way of the other ghosts and tripping them up because they were all too busy to notice that he was underfoot.

He was taking all the fun out of it for the rest of them, and at last they decided that it was too much to be borne. So they got up a petition to hand to the chief. It was a grand legal-looking paper having been drawn up by one of them who had been a solicitor in Glasgow before he happened to get to be a ghost. It stated their grievances against the discontented ghost and asked the chief to give his attention to relieving them.

The old chief was so put out when he got the petition that he turned two or three shades paler. He felt so queer that he even looked over his shoulder at the window to see if day was coming, although he knew quite well that it had just turned midnight. It really did upset him. The like of it had never happened to him before in one world or the other. So he sent for the discontented ghost and gave him the petition to read for himself.

'What's come over you lad?' roared the old chief. 'What do you mean by setting the clan and all by the ears! You're putting the place in such an uproar that we'll be getting a bad name.'

'It's not me,' said the young ghost sulkily. 'It's them. They're always going on at me about bracing up and being a proper ghost.'

'Well, why do you not do so then?' the old chief asked. 'That would stop them.'

'Because I don't want to be a ghost at all!' cried the discontented ghost. 'I never did want to be a ghost, either before or after I was one. I cannot thole it.'

The answer struck the old chief dumb. He'd never met such a thing before. He really didn't know what to say. But before he'd gathered his wits together the young ghost cried out in despair, 'Can't I be something else instead of a ghost? Is there not something you can do about it?'

The old chief had not headed two clans in two worlds without getting a very good knowledge of both human and ghost nature. This was not a matter he could settle by cajoling or arguing. He took a minute or two to think it over.

'Aye,' said the old chief at last. 'I'd not be saying that what you ask is impossible. But you'll have to understand that it's not myself that has the last word. I'll have to be getting permission. I'll do the best I can. Go along now, and be a good lad. I'll let you know.'

It was maybe a matter of a week before the chief sent for the discontented ghost again. 'Well, lad,' he said cheerfully, as soon as the young ghost came into the room. 'I'm to go ahead and find you something to suit you. I've been putting a lot of thought to the matter. How would it be if you just went back and were yourself again?'

"Well, I do not know about that,' said the young ghost doubtfully. 'After all, it's been a long time since I left and they've got used to me being gone. Besides, folks might not like the idea of me coming back to life again.'

'Och, they'd like it fine! They'd jump at the chance to have you back,' declared the old chief. 'But there's no need for haste. I'll tell you what to do. Just go and look things over on the quiet and see for yourself.'

So the young ghost did. He was back before the week was over.

The old chief greeted him hopefully. 'I'm thinking you'll want to be leaving soon for home again,' he said. 'We'll have to be getting you ready for it.'

'Och, nay!' the young ghost replied. ' 'Twould never do at all. They've let my next younger brother have my room, and he's moved all his things into it with mine. The room's so full it's a regular dustbin, but the lad's daft about it. You see, it's the first time he's had a room all to himself because there were so many of us at home. I'd not have the heart to go back and take it from him.

'Then there's my job. They've given that to the young fellow I was breaking in. Och, the lad's got a young wife and a new bairn. I'd not want to go back and take the job from him. 'Twould not be fair at all.'

13

'Was there not a lass you were thinking to marry?' asked the chief.

'You need not fash yourself about that,' said the young ghost with a smile. 'She'll be marrying my best friend soon. I'd not want to break that up.'

The old chief looked shocked.

'It's a very good thing,' the young ghost hastened to reassure him. 'You see, it's this way. When I was living there were things I never noticed about her, but being away and going back again I saw things that I'd never bothered about before. I'll grant you she's a bonny lass. They don't come bonnier. But she's an awful one to be talking. I can see now that she talks a lot too much, and she says such silly things. My friend doesn't seem to mind it, but I could never put up with it. I'd be glad to go back for the sake of my mother and my father. They'd welcome me back, for I know they love me and miss me. But it would bring trouble galore on them if I went back. What would the neighbours say? Besides, if something happened to me again, they'd just have all the grief of losing me to suffer all over. Nay, I'll not go back.'

'There's nothing we can do but put you in with somebody that's already in the world, then,' said the old chief. 'I'm warning you that it will not be comfortable at first, having to fit yourself in with somebody else. You'll be finding yourself feeling awful crowded until you get yourself used to it.'

'I'd not be minding that,' the young ghost said.

'Well, what would you have a fancy for?' asked the chief. But nothing he mentioned pleased the young

14

ghost. A doctor? They could probably find a doctor to tuck him into.

'Nay, you'll not do that!' the discontented ghost exclaimed. He knew all about doctors. His father was one. Up at all hours of the night, they were, with never a chance at a whole meal any day of their lives, and hardly time to get acquainted with their own bairns. He'd not want anything to do with the law, either, for he couldn't take it upon himself to decide who was right or wrong. Farmers were all right, and he'd always liked the countryside, but they led such lonely lives and worked too hard. Being a schoolmaster wouldn't be too bad. He'd always liked bairns and had hoped to have half a dozen of his own. But a schoolmaster was always having to make his lads do things they didn't want, like being quiet and sitting on hard benches and not squirming around. Besides masters and lads seldom could make friends with each other. It was as if there were a wall between them and neither could get over to the other side.

Well, that was the way it went, with the old chief mentioning one thing after another, and the young ghost turning each suggestion down. At last the old chief suggested wearily, 'Maybe you'd fancy being a financier?'

The young ghost brightened up. 'That might suit me fine,' he cried. 'It would be grand to have money galore. But I'd like to go and make sure I'd like it before I decided.'

'Go on, then,' said the old chief, thankful to be rid of him for a time at least.

15

But the discontented ghost was back in a day or two.

'There couldn't be anything worse!' he told the chief. 'Making a lot of money is fine enough, but the men who make it have to be running around so hard all day making it, and then they lie awake all night worrying about losing it, so it ends up with their getting dyspepsia and nervous headaches and the like till they go nearly daft. I'd not be suited at all with that sort of life.'

'Well, I've nothing more to offer,' said the old chief. 'I've reached my wits' end. Can you not think of anything yourself?'

'I'd not be saying I can at the moment,' the young ghost replied. 'But I'll try. I'll go and look round a bit.' And he went away, leaving the old chief feeling so glad to see him go that he felt like a new ghost.

It was quite a long time before he came back again and the old chief had to look at him a couple of times before he recognised him. The air of discontent had dropped from him entirely and he was as joyful as any ghost could be.

'I've got it!' he cried. ''Tis just the place for me!'

'Good!' the old chief exclaimed. 'And what is it, then?'

'I want to be a cat!' announced the young ghost.

'A *cat*!' The old chief couldn't believe his ears.

'Aye, a *cat*.' And looking into the old chief's face the young ghost begged, 'Och, do not tell me I cannot! I've set my heart upon it.'

'Och, nay!' The old chief hastened to say. ' 'Tis

not that it can't be done. To be sure though, a cat's an awful wee bit of a thing and it may take some trouble to fit you into it, but we could do it. As long as you're sure it's what you want.'

'I'm sure enough. What's more, I know well the very cat I want to be,' said the young ghost.

He led the old chief down through the streets of the town to a house that stood on a quiet square. They went into the house and up into a bedroom. The room was dark except for a lamp that stood on a table near the bed. There was a wee lad in the bed. He had been very ill and had got over his illness, but there was so little interest in life left in him that he just lay quietly and patiently, and there seemed to be nothing that could rouse him at all. His mother and father watched him from either side of the bed, keeping their eyes upon his face and hoping he'd show some notice of them. The young ghost paid no attention to the people in the room. He led the chief to the foot of the bed and pointed to a kitten that lay there sleeping on the blanket, curled up into a small furry ball.

'That's it,' he said. 'It wandered up here from the Broomielaw yesterday and they took it in and brought it up here to see if the bairn would like it. There's nine good lives in that wee body and it has the makings of a grand cat in it. That's the cat for me!'

The old chief said not a word, but he rolled up the sleeves of his shroud and, raising his bony arms, began making passes over the head of the young ghost.

The mother and father never noticed the two ghosts standing at the foot of the bed. And presently

17

There never was a kitten so petted and spoiled before

there was only one ghost there. The young ghost was gone. The old chief turned from the bed and went away.

Then the young ghost, as soon as he knew that he was all in the kitten, and really *was* the kitten himself, with four fine legs to leap about on and two fine ears to twitch and a fine long tail to swish, was so full of joy and delight that he began to dance at the foot of the bed. The thumping of the kitten's feet drew the lad's attention. He stirred and opened his eyes and looked at the kitten as it leapt and twisted and turned. The lad watched for a minute and the light came back into his eyes. He pulled himself up on his pillow and sat and pointed at the dancing kitten. And he laughed! 'Twas a weak sort of laugh and hardly worth the name, but it was a happy one. The kitten was the first thing he'd taken notice of for weeks and he was enchanted with it!

The bairn's mother caught the kitten up and kissed it on its little black nose and the bairn's father rang for the cook and told her to bring it a bowl of cream. The doctor came and said that undoubtedly the kitten had saved the lad's life. There never was a kitten so petted and spoiled before.

The lad grew better and better and after a while was well and went out again to play with his companions. The cat grew bigger and bigger and became a most rampraring and uproarious young tomcat. He was adored by all the tabby cats for miles around and was the terror of all the other tomcats in the town. He lost one of his ears and the tip of his tail and eight of his lives in battle, but he was always careful to save the ninth life so as to be having one for his old age.

And when at last he died, full of years and still pampered and cossetted because of the ancient service he had done the family when he saved the bairn's life, he gave up his last life most contentedly and willingly.

That was because of something he had known about cats from the very beginning. Since they are given nine lives to live, they live them all out in this world. Cats don't have ghosts!

THE KEEPERS OF THE WALL

By WILLIAM CROFT DICKINSON

'I SEE that someone has discovered a number of skeletons beneath the foundations of a wall and has brought forward the old idea that they were put there so that their ghosts could hold up the wall.'

'And why not?' interposed Henderson. 'It was long thought that burying a body under a wall would help to hold the wall secure.'

'Didn't Gordon Childe find something like that at Skara Brae?' queried Drummond.

'Yes,' Henderson confirmed. 'He found the skeletons of two old women at the foot of one of the walls; but he made only a suggestion that possibly they had been buried there so that their ghosts could hold up the wall. A guess, if you like. But a good guess.'

'I could tell you of a much more modern instance,' put in Robson, our new Professor of Mediæval Archæology. And I noticed that he spoke hesitantly. 'A sixteenth-century instance. Ghosts to hold up a wall. Perhaps even ghosts to gather the living to help them in their task,' he added slowly. 'Don't ask me to explain what I mean by that. I just don't know. All I know is that recently I had a terrifying experience on

21

the west coast—an experience that still makes me frightened of visiting ancient ruins by night.'

'I once had a terrifying experience myself,' said Drummond, quietly. 'You'll find at least one listener who'll understand. And the oftener you tell a tale, the less it haunts you.'

'Well, perhaps I'll find some of your relief, Drummond, by telling you the story of my night in the castle of Dunross—in March of this year, just before I came to Edinburgh to take up my chair.'

As you probably know, Dunross is one of a small group of interesting twelfth-century stone castles on the western seaboard. Only one of its sea-walls still stands, right up to the original wall-head (a feature which I now know only too well); the other two sea-walls have fallen down the cliff in a cascade of stones to the sea. The remaining wall, the landward wall, is little more than a few feet high, ruined and broken, though in it there is an entrance-gate with the remains of a stone stairway that undoubtedly rose up to the wall-walk. The better-known and better-preserved castles of Kisimul, Mingary and Tioram, each of them, like Dunross, perched on a sea rock, follow much the same plan; and I had a theory that the siting, the plan, and the constructional details of all four were so closely related that they bespoke the work of one particular school of military architects. Because of that, I had decided to make a careful examination of Dunross to confirm my belief that it fitted into the general plan of the group.

Right at the start I was fortunate enough to find a

crofter living by himself in a good-sized house some two or three miles from the castle. He had more than one room to spare, and he was more than willing to put me up. Moreover, he seemed to take a keen interest in my work, and came to join me every evening so that we could go home from Dunross together. And, as we walked back to his house, I would burden him with architectural details in which, as I was to learn in the end, he took no interest whatsoever.

I had appreciated his regular evening call, and had looked upon it as a friendly act. I had also appreciated our regular walk home. But when, on the night prior to my departure, I told him I would have to make one last visit to the castle in order to check a detail of the entrance-gate which I had not entered clearly enough in my note-book, I discovered he had had a definite reason of his own for calling to pick me up at the end of each day's work.

'You will not be going to Dunross in the night?' he asked, as I prepared to set out.

'Why, yes,' I replied. 'I just want to check a detail of the entrance-gate. I'll soon be back; and I have a torch. But don't wait up for me.'

'You cannot go there after dark,' he replied, fiercely. 'It would be madness. You would not come back. The wall would shut you in.'

I looked at him with astonishment. 'The wall would shut me in,' I repeated, lamely.

'Just so,' he answered. 'And for why would you think I have brought you away every evening as the darkness was closing in? Was it not to make sure you would not be kept there, like the rest of them? Shut in by the wall, to help to hold it firm.'

'To hold what wall firm? And how?' I asked, more mystified still. 'And who are "the rest", anyway?'

'You did not know, then?'

I shook my head.

'It is the ghosts of the MacLeods,' he replied. 'And since you do not know, I must tell you what way it is.'

And thereupon he told me a strange tale that, away back in the past, when there was a long-standing feud between the MacLeods and the Mac-Donalds of Clanranald, the MacDonalds had seized a birlinn, manned by MacLeods, and had brought the boat and their prisoners to Dunross. It was a time when MacDonald himself was rebuilding one of the sea-walls of his castle. So what did MacDonald do? Some of the MacLeods were just thrown into the dungeons, and left to starve there till they died; but six of them, fine strong fellows, were buried at the foot of MacDonald's new wall so that their ghosts would hold it secure. And that, I was told, was the one sea-wall which still stood, with never a stone that had fallen from it. Had I not seen it for myself? The other walls were ruined and tumbled down. But the ghosts of the six MacLeods would always hold that one sea-wall secure and strong.

'Well, that may be so,' I answered, when he had finished. 'But I still don't see why it should be dangerous to go to Dunross by night. As long as those ghosts are holding up the wall it can hardly fall down on me.'

'May be so!' he repeated, his eyes flashing. 'I tell you, man, it is so. No one has gone to Dunross by night and returned again. The MacLeods are wearying of their work and aye seeking others to share with them the burden of the wall.'

'And so evening visitors have been compelled to stay on,' I rejoined. And probably there was a little banter in my tone.

'I have told you the tale of it,' he replied, with Highland dignity. 'My father knew it, and his father before him. And, for a truth, they told me of two men who did not return. One, I mind, was a shepherd, seeking a ewe that had strayed; the other was a young man like yourself, who had come from the south and who would not be believing in ghosts and in walls that could shut a man in.'

With that parting shot he left me, to attend to some small task of his own. I could see that my disbelief had offended him, but I knew that the hurt would soon pass. But what of his tale? Of course I didn't believe it. And yet, for a brief space, I did hesitate about my final visit to Dunross. In the end I decided to go. Walls simply did not shut one in; and probably every Scottish castle had its ghost. Moreover, I did not want to leave without checking that detail of the entrance-gate.

'A typical legend,' I muttered to myself as I slipped on my oilskin. I felt my torch in my pocket. I had that, anyway. I opened the door quietly and stepped out into the night.

I must admit that as I walked along the rough track

that led to Dunross I was by no means as carefree as I would have been had my host not told his tale. I was ready to start at every shadow, and when, at last, I saw the dim outline of the ruined castle ahead of me, I stopped and very nearly turned back. But that reference to the 'young man from the south who did not believe in ghosts' acted as a challenge. I would go on and check that detail of the entrance-gate. More than that, I would go up to MacDonald's sea-wall, give it a resounding slap with my hand, say 'Goodbye' to the ghosts of the MacLeods, and then return to my host and tell him what I had done.

I walked boldly up to the castle. With the aid of my torch I studied the detail of the ruined entrance-gate. Then, sitting down on the grass, I propped my torch against a stone and made the necessary additional drawings in my note-book. By the time I had finished, all my misgivings had passed. I got up, shone my torch ahead of me, and marched boldly through the entrance-gate, across the castle-court, and straight up to the one high-standing and unbroken sea-wall.

'So much for ghosts,' I said aloud, as I stood a few feet from the wall, playing my torch up and down its length. And, at that very instant, my torch went out.

It would be idle to pretend that I was not frightened. I half-turned, and was on the point of running back to the entrance-gate, when I pulled myself together. A wall was a wall, and nothing more. Moreover, although the night was not completely black, I realized that I might easily stumble over one or more of the many fallen stones in the castle-court—and possibly sprain an ankle, perhaps even break a leg. And what should I do then?

'Don't be a fool,' I remember saying to myself. 'Have a look at your torch.'

The battery had given no previous indication that it was running down. Probably there was simply a faulty contact. I struck the torch gently against the palm of my hand. Nothing happened. Somewhat anxiously I struck it this way and that, again and again. Still it refused to work. The answer could only be that the filament in the bulb had broken. 'Damn the thing,' I said, and stuffed it back into my pocket. I would have to crawl on all fours to the entrance-gate. Safer that way. And I would get some assistance from the faint light in the sky.

Then I remembered my matches! I opened the box carefully and felt inside. Good! There were quite a number left. Certainly enough to light my way through the fallen stones. And there was no wind.

I took out a match and struck it; but it failed to light. Thinking I had struck the wrong end of the match, I turned it round in my fingers and again struck it on the box. Still no light came. Throwing the match away, I took out another. Again the match refused to light. Frenziedly, and with shaking hands, I tried match after match, but not one would strike. I came to the last match of all. I prayed that it would strike. But there was still the same hard scrape on the sandpaper of the box, and no welcome blaze of light.

After that, it is difficult to tell you what happened. To say that I was now frightened would be an understatement. I was terrified. Yet somehow I still kept myself under control. Almost as soon as I had thrown away my last match I dropped down on to my hands and knees, turned my back to the wall, and began to crawl away as fast as I could. In that way, I assured myself, I was bound to find the entrance-gate in time. And pray heaven it would not take long.

I had crawled perhaps twenty yards when I came to fallen stones. That meant I was now well away from the wall. I looked up, hoping to see the low ruins of the landward-wall silhouetted against the sky. Instead, I saw in front of me the high-towering unbroken sea-wall from which I had fled.

At once I turned and crawled away in the opposite direction. Smooth turf! Fallen stones! Ah! I was away this time. And this time, as I looked up, slowly and fearfully, again I saw the sea-wall barring my way.

With that, I'm not ashamed to say that all my control went. For some reason or other—possibly a subconscious fear of disabling myself on the fallen stones—I did not stand up and run. I scurried on all fours, first this way, then that, constantly looking for the escape that would be offered by the broken outline of the landward-wall and as constantly only seeing the high unbroken sea-wall in front of me.

How long that lasted I do not know. I had lost all sense of time. Perhaps I had lost all reason too. All I know is that, in the end, bruised, weary, and utterly worn out, I sat down. I was resigned to my fate. If the wall had to close in upon me, if I had to disappear as the others had done, well, let it be so. I could do no more.

And then, when all hope had gone, even when all desire had gone with it, I heard the sound of crunching stones. This was the end. It came almost as a relief. But, strangely, no stones crushed me. I suffered no entombment, no agony in which I fought for breath. Instead, a bright light suddenly burned on my closed and waiting eyes. What did this final torture mean?

Summoning up all the last dregs of courage that were left in me, I opened my eyes, slowly, wearily, painfully. The light dazzled me. Then, with a queer feeling that I didn't know whether to shout, or to laugh, or to cry, I realised that I was in the beam from the headlights of a car—headlights that were shining through the entrance-gate, and shining straight on to me. I heard a shout; then another. Seconds later, I was literally carried out of the castle and gently lifted into the car. Someone poured a stiff whisky down my throat. And a blessed unconsciousness came to me.

The next morning I awoke in my own bed. My host, the crofter, was sitting on a chair by the bedside. He must have heard me move, for he stood up and bent over me.

'You'll be feeling fine now,' he said, half in question, half in affirmation.

I looked up at him, my wits slowly recovering.

'I am glad you came,' I said, slowly. 'I was all in, and ready to die. It seemed as though the wall would never let me go.'

'Praised be the Lord, but we cheated it. The doctor

and I. The two of us. No less. For I had not the boldness to be seeking you at Dunross by my own self.'

There was the sound of a car outside.

'And there's the doctor, now,' he cried, striding quickly to the door.

The doctor was middle-aged, keen-eyed, and carrying himself like an athlete.

'So here is the young man who doesn't believe in ghosts,' he said cheerily, as he came over to my bed. 'Don't know that I do myself. Can't be sure.'

He took my wrist and felt the beating of my pulse.

'Not bad at all,' he said. 'Fine, in fact, for the morning after the night before. Did I say I didn't believe in ghosts? Or do I? Don't know. Yet I doubt if I'd go to Dunross by night. Save when called out on duty, of course.'

His eyes were twinkling, and his whole manner was a tonic and restorative.

'Tell me now,' he continued, 'what happened to ye before we picked ye up. And once we were carrying ye to my car, there ye were, sobbing like an unhappy child.'

'I didn't know that,' I replied.

'It helps, man. It helps. Washes away the worries. But what happened to ye?'

Haltingly I told him of the sudden failure of my torch, of the matches that would not strike, and of the wall always in front of me, always shutting me in.

'So,' he said, when I had finished. 'So that is the way of it. I've often wondered what those dead Macleods did to their evening visitors. But man, I suspect

30

ye were just crawling in circles. 'Tis easy enough. And easier still when terror gets hold of ye. Have ye ever tried to find the door of a room, in the black-out, when the bombs started dropping down?'

'But my torch!' I cried. 'My matches!'

'Do ye put spent matches back into the box, tidy-like, instead of throwing them away?' he asked.

Here was a thought that sobered me. But it was impossible.

'Yes,' I admitted, grudgingly. 'But only occasion-ally. There could not possibly be more than two or three spent matches in the box at any time. And even if all the matches were spent ones—and I'm con-vinced they were not—what of my torch? Why did that fail, too?"

'Let me look at it,' he said.

'It will be in the pocket of my oilskin,' I replied, raising myself up and looking around the room. 'There, on the peg by the door.'

He walked over to my oilskin and took out the torch. He pressed the switch, and at once the torch shone bright and clear.

For a moment or two he hummed a tune to him-self. He tried the torch a second time; and once more it lit at his touch.

'So,' he said again. 'Yet I've known the horn on my car fail to sound one day and sound like the last trump on the day following.'

Again he hummed his tune as he played with my torch in his hand. Then the movement of his hand slackened. The humming ceased. He dropped the torch

31

on a chair and turned to me. And this time there was a different look in his eyes.

'Man, but I'm afraid,' he said, slowly. 'We've been playing with explanations because we feared the circumstance. Did I say I would not go to Dunross by night? I doubt I shall not be going to Dunross by day, either. To be frank with ye, I dare not go. I dare not go, lest I should find there an answer that is no answer—lest I should find a cluster of live matches lying there, at the foot of the wall.'

FIDDLER, PLAY FAST, PLAY FASTER

By Ruth Sawyer

IT IS a strange island and an enchanted one—our Isle of Man. It took many a thousand years and more before mankind discovered it, it being well-known that the spirits of water, of earth, of air and fire did put on an enchantment, hiding it with a blue flame of mist, so that it could not be seen by mortal eye. The mist was made out of the heat of a great fire and the salt vapour of the sea and it covered the island like a bank of clouds. Then one day the fire was let out, the sea grew quiet, and lo, the land stood out in all its height of mountains and ruggedness of coast, its green of fens and rushing of waterfalls. Sailors passing saw it. And from that day forth men came to it and much of its enchantment was lost.

But not all. At all seasons of the year there are spirits abroad on the Isle, working their charms and making their mischief. And there is on the coast, overhanging the sea, a great cavern reaching below the earth, out of which the Devil comes when it pleases him, to walk where he will upon the Isle. A wise Manxman does not go far without a scrap of iron or a lump of salt in his pocket; and if it is night, likely, he will have stuck in his cap a sprig of rowan and a sprig of wormwood, feather from a seagull's wing and skin from a conger eel. For these keep away evil spirits; and who upon the Isle would meet with evil, or who would give himself foolishly into its power?

So it is that in the south upon the ramparts of Castle Rushen the cannon are mounted on stone crosses above the ramparts; and when a south Manxman knocks at his neighbour's door he does not cry out: "Are you within?" But rather he asks: "Are there any sinners inside?" For evil is a fearsome thing and who would have traffic with it?

I am long beginning my tale, but some there may be who know little of our Isle and a storyteller cannot always bring his listeners by the straightest road to the story he has to tell. This one is of the south, where the mists hang the heaviest, where the huts are built of turf and thatched with broom, where the cattle are small and the goats many, and where a farmer will tell you he has had his herd brought to fold by the fenodyree—a goblin that is half goat, half boy. But that is another tale.

Let me begin with an old Manx saying—it tunes the story well: "When a poor man helps another, God in His Heaven laughs with delight." This shows you that the men of Man are kind to one another, and God is not far from them even when the Devil walks abroad.

Count a hundred years, and as many more as you like, and you will come to the time of my story.

Beyond Castletown in the sheading of Kirk Christ Rushen lived, then, a lump of a lad named Billy Nell Kewley. He could draw as sweet music from the fiddle as any fiddler of Man. When the Christmas-time began, he was first abroad with his fiddle. Up the glens and over the fens, fiddling for this neighbour and that as the night ran out, calling the hour and crying the weather, that those snug on their beds of chaff would know before the day broke what kind of day it would be making. Before Yule he started his fiddling, playing half out of the night and half into the day, playing this and playing that, carrying with him, carefully in his cap, the sprig of rowan and the sprig of wormwood, with the iron and salt in the pocket of his brown woollen breeches. And there you have Billy Nell Kewley on the Eve of Saint Fingan.

Now over Castletown on a high building of cliff rises Castle Rushen. Beyond stands the oldest monastery on the Isle, in ruin these hundreds of years, Rushen Abbey, with its hundred treens of land. It was through the Forest of Rushen Billy Nell was coming on Saint Thomas's Eve, down the Glen to the Quiggan hut, playing the tune "Andisop" and whistling a running of notes to go with it. He broke the whistle, ready to call the hour: "Two of the morning," and the weather: "Cold—with a mist over all," when he heard the running of feet behind him in the dark.

Quick as a falcon he reached for the sprig in his cap. It was gone; the pushing through the green boughs of the forest had torn it. He quickened his own feet. Could it be a buggan after him—an ugly, evil one, a fiend of Man who cursed mortals and bore malice against them, who would bring a body to perdition and then laugh at him? Billy Nell's feet went fast—went faster.

But his ear, dropping behind him, picked up the sound of other feet; they were going fast—and faster. Could it be the fenodyree—the hairy one? That would be not so terrible. The fenodyree played pranks, but he, having once loved a human maid, did not bring evil to humans. And he lived, if the ancient ones could be believed, in Glen Rushen.

And then a voice spoke out of the blackness. "Stop, I command!"

What power lay in that voice! It brought the feet of Billy Nell to a stop—for all he wanted them to go on, expected them to keep running. Afterwards he was remembering the salt and iron in his pocket he might have thrown between himself and what followed so closely after him out of the mist. But he did nothing but stop—stop and say to himself: "Billy Nell Kewley, could it be the Noid ny Hanmey who commands—the Enemy of the Soul?" And he stood stock still in the darkness too frightened to shiver, for it was the Devil himself he was thinking of.

He who spoke appeared, carrying with him a kind of reddish light that came from everywhere and nowhere, a light the colour of fever, or heat lightning, or of the very pit of Hell. But when Billy Nell looked he saw as fine a gentleman as ever had come to Man —fine and tall, grave and stern, well clothed in knee breeches and silver buckles and lace and such finery. He spoke with grace and grimness: "Billy Nell Kewley of Castletown, I have heard you are a monstrous good fiddler. No one better, so they say."

"I play fair, sir," said Billy Nell modestly.

"I would have you play for me. Look!" He dipped into a pocket of his breeches and drawing out a hand so white, so tapering, it might have been a lady's, he showed Billy Nell gold pieces. And in the reddish light that came from everywhere and nowhere Billy saw the strange marking on them. "You shall have as many of these as you can carry away with you if you will fiddle for me and my company three nights from tonight," said the fine one.

"And where shall I fiddle?" asked Billy Nell Kewley.

"I will send a messenger for you, Billy Nell; half-way up the Glen he will meet you. This side of midnight he will meet you."

"I will come," said the fiddler, for he had never heard of so much gold—to be his for a night's fiddling. And being not half so fearful he began to shiver. At that moment a cock crew far away, a bough brushed his eyes, the mist hung about him like a cloak, and he was alone. Then he ran, ran to Quiggan's hut, calling the hour: "Three of the clock," crying the weather: "Cold with a heavy mist."

The next day he counted, did Billy Nell Kewley, counted the days up to three and found that the night he was to fiddle for all the gold he could carry with him was Christmas Eve. A kind or terror took hold of him. What manner of spirit was the Enemy of the Soul? Could he be anything he chose to be—a devil in Hell or a fine gentleman on Earth? He ran about asking everyone, and everyone gave him a different answer. He went to the monks of the Abbey and found them working in their gardens, their black cowls thrown back from their faces, their bare feet treading the brown earth.

The Abbot came, and dour enough he looked. "Shall I go, your reverence? Shall I fiddle for one I know not? Is it good gold he is giving me?" asked Billy Nell.

"I cannot answer any one of those questions," said the Abbot. "That night alone can give the answers: Is the gold good or cursed? Is the man noble or is he the Devil? But go. Carry salt, carry iron and bollan bane. Play a dance and watch. Play another—and watch. Then play a Christmas hymn and see!"

This side of midnight, Christmas Eve, Billy Nell Kewley climbed the Glen, his fiddle wrapped in a lamb's fleece to keep out the wet. Mist, now blue, now red, hung over the blackness, so thick he had to feel his way along the track with his feet, stumbling.

He passed where Castle Rushen should have stood. He passed on, was caught up and carried as by the mist and in it. He felt his feet leave the track, he felt them gain it again. And then the mist rolled back like clouds after a storm and before him he saw such a splendid sight as no lump of a lad had ever beheld before. A castle, with courtyard and corridors, with piazzas and high roofings, spread before him all a-glowing with light. Windows wide and doorways wide, and streaming with the light came laughter. And there was his host more splendid than all, with velvet and satin, silver and jewels. About him moved what Billy Nell took to be high-born lords and ladies, come from overseas no doubt, for never had he seen their like on Man.

In the middle of the great hall he stood, unwrapping his fiddle, sweetening the strings, rosining the bow, limbering his fingers. The laughter died. His host shouted:

"Fiddler, play fast—play faster!"

In all his life and never again did Billy Nell play as he played that night. The music of his fiddle made the music of a hundred fiddles. About him whirled the dancers like crazy rainbows: blue and orange, purple and yellow, green and red all mixed together until his head swam with the colour. And yet the sound of the dancers' feet was the sound of the grass growing or the corn ripening or the holly reddening —which is to say no sound at all. Only there was the sound of his playing, and above that the sound of his host shouting, always shouting:

"Fiddler, play fast—play faster!"

Ever faster—ever faster! It was as with a mighty wind Billy Nell played now, drawing the wild, mad music from his fiddle. He played tunes he had never heard before, tunes which cried and shrieked and howled and sighed and sobbed and cried out in pain.

"Play fast—play faster!"

He saw one standing by the door—a monk in a black cowl, barefooted, a monk who looked at him with deep, sad eyes and held two fingers of his hand to his lips as if to hush the music.

Then, and not till then, did Billy Nell Kewley remember what the Abbot had told him. But the monk —how came he here? And then he remembered that, too. A tale so old it had grown ragged with the telling, so that only a scrap here and there was left: how long ago, on the blessed Christmas Eve, a monk had slept through the Midnight Mass to the Virgin and to the new-born Child, and how, at complin on Christmas Day, he was missing and never seen again. The ancient ones said that the Devil had taken him away, that Enemy of All Souls, had stolen his soul because he had slept over Mass.

Terror left Billy Nell. He swept his bow so fast over the strings of his fiddle that his eyes could not follow it.

"Fiddler, play fast—play faster!"

"Master, I play faster and faster!" He moved his own body to the mad music, moved it across the hall to the door where stood the monk. He crashed out the last notes; on the floor at the feet of the monk he dropped iron, salt, and bollan bane. Then out of the silence he drew the notes of a Christmas carol—softly, sweetly it rose on the air:

> Adeste fideles, laeti triumphantes,
> Venite, venite in Bethlehem:
> Natum videte, Regem angelorum:
> Venite adoremus, venite adoremus,
> Venite adoremus—Dominum.

Racked were the ears of Billy Nell at the sounds which surged above the music, groans and wailing, the agony of souls damned. Racked were his eyes with the sights he saw: the servants turned to fleshless skeletons, the lords and ladies to howling demons. And the monk with the black cowl and bare feet sifted down to the grass beneath the vanishing castle—a heap of gray dust. But in the dust shone one small spark of holy light—a monk's soul, freed. And Billy Nell took it in his hand and tossed it high in the wind as one tosses a falcon to the sky for free passage. And he watched it go its skimming way until the sky gathered it in.

Billy Nell Kewley played his way down the Glen, stopping to call the hour: "Three of this blessed Christmas Morning," stopping to cry the weather: "The sky is clear . . . the Christ is born."

THE MAGIC SHOP

By H. G. WELLS

I HAD seen the Magic Shop from afar several times; I had passed it once or twice, a shop window of alluring little objects, magic balls, magic hens, wonderful cones, ventriloquist dolls, the material of the basket trick, packs of cards that *looked* all right, and all that sort of thing, but never had I thought of going in until one day, almost without warning, Gip hauled me by my finger right up to the window, and so conducted himself that there was nothing for it but to take him in. I had not thought the place was there, to tell the truth—a modest-sized frontage in Regent Street, between the picture shop and the place where the chicks run about just out of patent incubators—but there it was sure enough. I had fancied it was down nearer the Circus, or round the corner in Oxford Street, or even in Holborn; always over the way and a little inaccessible it had been, with something of the mirage in its position; but here it was now quite indisputably, and the fat end of Gip's pointed finger made a noise upon the glass.

"If I was rich," said Gip, dabbing a finger at the

Disappearing Egg. "I'd buy myself that. And that" —which was The Crying Baby, Very Human—"and that," which was a mystery, and called, so a neat card asserted, "Buy One and Astonish Your Friends."

"Anything," said Gip, "will disappear under one of those cones. I have read about it in a book.

"And there, dadda, is the Vanishing Halfpenny— only they've put it this way up so's we can't see how it's done."

Gip, dear boy, inherits his mother's breeding, and he did not propose to enter the shop or worry in any way; only, you know, quite unconsciously, he lugged my finger doorward, and he made his interest clear.

"That," he said, and pointed to the Magic Bottle.

"If you had that?" I said; at which promising inquiry he looked up with a sudden radiance.

"I could show it to Jessie," he said, thoughtful as ever of others.

"It's less than a hundred days to your birthday, Gibbles," I said, and laid my hand on the door-handle.

Gip made no answer, but his grip tightened on my finger, and so we came into the shop.

It was no common shop this; it was a magic shop, and all the prancing precedence Gip would have taken in the matter of mere toys was wanting. He left the burden of the conversation to me.

It was a little, narrow shop, not very well lit, and the door-bell pinged again with a plaintive note as we closed it behind us. For a moment or so we were alone and could glance about us. There was a tiger in papier-mâché on the glass case that covered the low counter—a grave, kind-eyed tiger that waggled his

43

head in a methodical manner; there were several crystal spheres, a china hand holding magic cards, a stock of magic fish-bowls in various sizes, and an immodest magic hat that shamelessly displayed its springs. On the floor were magic mirrors; one to draw you out long and thin, one to swell your head and vanish your legs, and one to make you short and fat like a draught; and while we were laughing at these the shopman, as I suppose, came in.

At any rate, there he was behind the counter—a curious, sallow, dark man, with one ear larger than the other and a chin like the toe-cap of a boot.

"What can we have the pleasure?" he said, spreading his long magic fingers on the glass case; and so with a start we were aware of him.

"I want," I said, "to buy my little boy a few simple tricks."

"Legerdemain?" he asked. "Mechanical? Domestic?"

"Anything amusing?" said I.

"Um!" said the shopman, and scratched his head for a moment as if thinking. Then, quite distinctly, he drew from his head a glass ball. "Something in this way?" he said, and held it out.

The action was unexpected. I had seen the trick done at entertainments endless times before—it's part of the common stock of conjurers—but I had not expected it here.

"That's good," I said, with a laugh.

"Isn't it?" said the shopman.

Gip stretched out his disengaged hand to take this object and found merely a blank palm.

The shopman smiled at Gyp. "It's only the Right Sort of Boy gets through that doorway," he said.

"It's in your pocket," said the shopman, and there is was!

"How much will that be?" I asked.

"We make no charge for glass balls," said the shopman politely. "We get them"—he picked one out of his elbow as he spoke—"free." He produced another from the back of his neck, and laid it beside its predecessor on the counter. Gip regarded his glass ball sagely, then directed a look of inquiry at the two on the counter, and finally brought his round-eyed scrutiny to the shopman, who smiled. "You may have those two," said the shopman, "and if you *don't* mind one from my mouth. *So!*"

Gip counselled me mutely for a moment, and then in a profound silence put away the four balls, resumed my reassuring finger, and nerved himself for the next event.

"We get all our smaller tricks in that way," the shopman remarked.

I laughed in the manner of one who subscribes to a jest. "Instead of going to the wholesale shop," I said. "Of course, it's cheaper."

"In a way," the shopman said. "Though we pay in the end. But not so heavily—as people suppose. . . . Our larger tricks, and our daily provisions and all the other things we want, we get out of that hat. . . . And you know, sir, if you'll excuse my saying it, there *isn't* a wholesale shop, not for Genuine Magic goods, sir. I don't know if you noticed our inscription—the Genuine Magic Shop." He drew a business card from his cheek and handed it to me. "Genuine," he said, with his finger on the word, and added. "There is absolutely no deception, sir."

He seemed to be carrying out the joke pretty thoroughly, I thought.

He turned to Gip with a smile of remarkable affability. "You, you know, are the Right Sort of Boy."

I was surprised at his knowing that, because, in the interests of discipline, we keep it rather a secret even at home; but Gip received it in unflinching silence, keeping a steadfast eye on him.

"It's only the Right Sort of Boy gets through that doorway."

And, as if by way of illustration, there came a rattling at the door, and a squeaking little voice could be faintly heard. "Nyar! I *warn* 'a go in there, dadda, I WARN 'a go in there. Ny-a-a-ah!" and then the accents of a downtrodden parent, urging consolations and propitiations. "It's locked, Edward," he said.

"But it isn't," said I.

"It is, sir," said the shopman, "always—for that sort of child," and as he spoke we had a glimpse of the other youngster, a little white face, pallid from sweet-eating and over-sapid food, and distorted by evil passions, a ruthless little egotist, pawing at the enchanted pane.

"It's no good, sir," said the shopman, as I moved, with my natural helpfulness, doorward, and presently the spoilt child was carried off howling.

"How do you manage that?" I said, breathing a little more freely.

"Magic!" said the shopman, with a careless wave

of the hand, and behold! sparks of coloured fire flew out of his fingers and vanished into the shadows of the shop.

"You were saying," he said, addressing himself to Gip, "before you came in, that you would like one of our 'Buy One and Astonish your Friends' boxes?"

Gip, after a gallant effort, said "Yes."

"It's in your pocket."

And leaning over the counter—he really had an extraordinary long body—this amazing person produced the article in the customary conjurer's manner. "Paper," he said, and took a sheet out of the empty hat with the springs; "string," and behold his mouth was a string box, from which he drew an unending thread, which when he tied his parcel he bit off— and it seemed to me, swallowed the ball of string. And then he lit a candle at the nose of one of the ventriloquist's dummies, stuck one of his fingers (which had become sealing-wax red) into the flame, and so sealed the parcel. "Then there was the Disappearing Egg," he remarked, and produced one from within my coat-breast and packed it, and also The Crying Baby, Very Human. I handed each parcel to Gip as it was ready, and he clasped them to his chest.

He said very little, but his eyes were eloquent; the clutch of his arms were eloquent. He was the playground of unspeakable emotions. These, you know, were *real* Magics.

Then, with a start, I discovered something moving about in my hat—something soft and jumpy. I whipped it off, and a ruffled pigeon—no doubt a confederate—dropped out and ran on the counter, and went, I fancy, into a cardboard box behind the papier-mâché tiger.

"Tut, tut!" said the shopman, dexterously relieving me of my headdress; "careless bird, and—as I live—nesting!"

He shook my hat, and shook out into his extended hand, two or three eggs, a large marble, a watch, about half a dozen of the inevitable glass balls, and then crumpled, crinkled paper, more and more and more, talking all the time of the way in which people neglect to brush their hats *inside* as well as out—politely, of course, but with a certain personal application. "All sorts of things accumulate, sir. . . . Not *you*, of course, in particular. . . . Nearly every customer. . . . Astonishing what they carry about with them. . . ." The crumpled paper rose and billowed on the counter more and more and more, until he was nearly hidden from us, until he was altogether hidden, and still his voice went on and on. "We none of us know what the fair semblance of a human being may conceal, sir. Are we all then no better than brushed exteriors, whited sepulchres——"

His voice stopped—exactly like when you hit a neighbour's gramophone with a well-aimed brick, the same instant silence—and the rustle of the paper stopped and everything was still. . . .

"Have you done with my hat?" I said, after an interval.

There was no answer.

I stared at Gip, and Gip stared at me, and there were our distortions in the magic mirrors, looking very rum, and grave, and quiet. . . .

"I think we'll go now," I said. "Will you tell me how much all this comes to? . . .

"I say," I said, on a rather louder note, "I want the bill; and my hat, please."

It might have been a sniff from behind the paper pile. . . .

"Let's look behind the counter, Gip," I said. "He's making fun of us."

I led Gip round the head-wagging tiger, and what do you think there was behind the counter? No one at all! Only my hat on the floor, and a common conjurer's lop-eared white rabbit lost in meditation, and looking as stupid and crumpled as only a conjurer's rabbit can do. I resumed my hat, and the rabbit lolloped a lollop or so out of my way.

"Dadda!" said Gip, in a guilty whisper.

"What is it, Gip?" said I.

"I *do* like this shop, dadda."

"So should I," I said to myself, "if the counter wouldn't suddenly extend itself to shut one off from the door." But I didn't call Gip's attention to that. "Pussy!" he said, with a hand out to the rabbit as it came lolloping past us; "Pussy, do Gip a magic!" and his eyes followed it as it squeezed through a door I had certainly not remarked a moment before. Then this door opened wider, and the man with one ear larger than the other appeared again. He was smiling still, but his eye met mine with something between amusement and defiance. "You'd like to see our showroom, sir," he said, with an innocent suavity. Gip tugged my finger forward. I glanced at the counter and met the shopman's eye again. I was beginning to think the magic just a little too genuine. "We haven't *very* much time," I said. But somehow we were inside the showroom before I could finish that.

"All goods of the same quality," said the shopman, rubbing his flexible hands together, "and that is the Best. Nothing in the place that isn't genuine Magic, and warranted thoroughly rum. Excuse me, sir!"

I felt him pull at something that clung to my coat-sleeve, and then I saw he held a little, wriggling red demon by the tail—the little creature bit and fought and tried to get at his hand—and in a moment he tossed it carelessly behind a counter. No doubt the thing was only an image of twisted indiarubber, but for the moment——! And his gesture was exactly that of a man who handles some petty biting bit of vermin. I glanced at Gip, but Gip was looking at a magic rocking-horse. I was glad he hadn't seen the thing. "I say," I said, in an undertone, and indicating Gip and the red demon with my eyes, "you haven't many things like *that* about, have you?"

"None of ours! Probably brought it with you," said the shopman—also in an undertone, and with a more dazzling smile than ever. "Astonishing what people *will* carry about with them unawares!" And then to Gip, "Do you see anything you fancy here?"

There were many things that Gip fancied there.

He turned to this astonishing tradesman with mingled confidence and respect. "Is that a Magic Sword?" he said.

"A Magic Toy Sword. It neither bends, breaks, nor cuts the fingers. It renders the bearer invincible in battle against any one under eighteen. Half a crown to seven and sixpence, according to size. These panoplies on cards are for juvenile knights-errant and very useful—shield of safety, sandals of swiftness, helmet of invisibility."

"Oh, dadda!" gasped Gip.

I tried to find out what they cost, but the shopman did not heed me. He had got Gip now; he had got him away from my finger; he had embarked upon the exposition of all his confounded stock, and nothing was going to stop him. Presently I saw with a qualm of distrust and something very like jealousy that Gip had hold of this person's fin．．r as usually he has hold of mine. No doubt the fellow was interesting, I thought, and had an interestingly faked lot of stuff. really *good* faked stuff, still——

I wandered after them, saying very little, but keeping an eye on this prestidigital fellow. After all, Gip was enjoying it. And no doubt when the time came to go we should be able to go quite easily.

It was a long, rambling place, that showroom, a gallery broken up by stands and stalls and pillars, with archways leading off to other departments, in which the queerest-looking assistants loafed and stared at one, and with perplexing mirrors and curtains. So perplexing, indeed, were these that I was presently unable to make out the door by which we had come.

The shopman showed Gip magic trains that ran without steam or clockwork, just as you, set the signals, and then some very, very, valuable boxes of soldiers that all came alive directly you took off the lid and said—I myself haven't a very quick ear, and it was a tongue-twisting sound, but Gip—he has his mother's ear—got it in no time. "Bravo!" said the shopman, putting the men back into the box unceremoniously and handing it to Gip. "Now," said the shopman, and in a moment Gip had made them all alive again.

"You'll take that box?" asked the shopman.

"We'll take that box," said I, "unless you charge its full value. In which case it would need a Trust Magnate——"

"Dear Heart! *No!*" and the shopman swept the little men back again, shut the lid, waved the box in the air, and there is was, in brown paper, tied up and—*with Gip's full name and address on the paper!*

The shopman laughed at my amazement.

"This is the genuine magic," he said. "The real thing."

"It's a little too genuine for my taste," I said again.

After that he fell to showing Gip tricks, odd tricks, and still odder the way they were done. He explained them, he turned them inside out, and there was the dear little chap nodding his busy bit of a head in the sagest manner.

I did not attend as well as I might. "Hey, presto!" said the Magic Shopman, and then would come the clear, small "Hey, presto!" of the boy. But I was distracted by other things. It was being borne in upon me just how tremendously rum this place was; it was, so to speak, inundated by a sense of rumness. There was something a little rum about the fixtures, even, about the ceiling, about the floor, about the casually distributed chairs. I had a queer feeling that whenever I wasn't looking at them they went askew, and moved about, and played a noiseless puss-in-the corner behind my back. And the cornice had a serpentine design with masks—masks altogether too expressive for proper plaster.

Then abruptly my attention was caught by one of the odd-looking assistants. He was some way off and evidently unaware of my presence—I saw a sort of three-quarter length of him over a pile of toys and through an arch—and, you know, he was leaning against a pillar in an idle sort of way doing the most horrid things with his features! The particular horrid thing he did was with his nose. He did it just as though he was idle and wanted to amuse himself. First of all it was a short, blobby nose, and then suddenly he shot it out like a telescope, and then out it flew and became thinner and thinner until it was like a long, red flexible whip. Like a thing in a nightmare it was! He flourished it about and flung it forth as a fly-fisher flings his line.

My instant thought was that Gip mustn't see him. I turned about, and there was Gip quite preoccupied with the shopman, and thinking no evil. They were whispering together and looking at me. Gip was standing on a little stool, and the shopman was holding a sort of big drum in his hand.

"Hide and seek, dadda!" cried Gip. "You're He!"

And before I could do anything to prevent it, the shopman had clapped the big drum over him.

I saw what was up directly. "Take that off," I cried, "this instant! You'll frighten the boy. Take it off!"

The shopman with the unequal ears did so without

a word, and held the big cylinder towards me to show its emptiness. And the little stool was vacant! In that instant, my boy had utterly disappeared! . . .

You know, perhaps, that sinister something that comes like a hand out of the unseen and grips your heart about. You know it take your common self away and leaves you tense and deliberate, neither slow nor hasty, neither angry nor afraid. So it was with me.

I came up to this grinning shopman and kicked his stool aside.

"Stop this folly!" I said. "Where is my boy?"

"You see," he said, still displaying the drum's interior, "there is no deception——"

I put out my hand to grip him, and he eluded me by a dexterous movement. I snatched again, and he turned from me and pushed open a door to escape. "Stop!" I said, and he laughed, receding. I leapt after him—into utter darkness.

Thud!

"Lor' bless my 'eart! I didn't see you coming, sir!"

I was in Regent Street, and I had collided with a decent-looking working man; and a yard away, perhaps, and looking a little perplexed with himself, was Gip. There was some sort of apology, and then Gip had turned and come to me with a bright little smile, as though for a moment he had missed me.

And he was carrying four parcels in his arm!

He secured immediate possession of my finger.

For a second I was rather at a loss. I stared round to see the door of the Magic Shop, and, behold, it was not there! There was no door, no shop, nothing, only the common pilaster between the shop where they sell pictures and the window with the chicks! . . .

I did the only thing possible in that mental tumult; I walked straight to the kerbstone and held up my umbrella for a cab.

" 'Ansoms," said Gip, in a note of culminating exultation.

I helped him in, recalled my address with an effort, and got in also. Something unusual proclaimed itself in my tail-coat pocket, and I felt and discovered a glass ball. With a petulant expression I flung it into the street.

Gip said nothing.

For a space neither of us spoke.

"Dadda!" said Gip at last, "that *was* a proper shop!"

I came round with that to the problem of just how the whole thing had seemed to him. He looked completely undamaged—so far, good; he was neither scared nor unhinged, he was simply tremendously satisfied with the afternoon's entertainment, and there in his arms were the four parcels

Confound it! what could be in them?

"Um!" I said. "Little boys can't go to shops like that every day."

He received this with his usual stoicism, and for a moment I was sorry I was his father and not his mother, and so couldn't suddenly there, *coram populo,* in our hansom, kiss him. After all, I thought, the thing wasn't so very bad.

But it was only when we opened the parcels that I really began to be reassured. Three of them contained boxes of soldiers, quite ordinary lead soldiers, but of so good quality as to make Gip altogether forget that originally these parcels had been Magic Tricks of the only genuine sort, and the fourth contained a kitten, a little living white kitten, in excellent health and appetite and temper.

I saw this unpacking with a sort of provisional relief. I hung about in the nursery for quite an unconscionable time. . . .

That happened six months ago. And now I am beginning to believe it is all right. The kitten had only the magic natural to all kittens, and the soldiers seemed as steady a company as any colonel could desire. And Gip——?

The intelligent parent will understand that I have to go cautiously with Gip.

But I went so far as this one day. I said, "How would you like your soldiers to come alive, Gip, and march about by themselves?"

"Mine do," said Gip. "I just have to say a word I know before I open the lid."

"Then they march about alone?"

"Oh, *quite*, dadda. I shouldn't like them if they didn't do that."

I displayed no unbecoming surprise, and since then I have taken occasion to drop in upon him once or twice, unannounced, when the soldiers were about, but so far I have never discovered them performing in anything like a magical manner. . . .

It's so difficult to tell.

There's also a question of finance. I have an incurable habit of paying bills. I have been up and down Regent Street several times looking for that shop. I am inclined to think, indeed, that in that matter honour is satisfied, and that, since Gip's name and address are known to them, I may very well leave it to these people, whoever they may be, to send in their bill in their own time.

MR FOX

A Traditional English Folk Story

LADY MARY was young, and Lady Mary was fair. She had two brothers, and more lovers than she could count. But of them all, the bravest and most gallant, was a Mr Fox, whom she met when she was down at her father's country house. No one knew who Mr Fox was, but he was certainly brave, and surely rich, and of all her lovers, Lady Mary cared for him alone. At last it was agreed upon between them that they should be married. Lady Mary asked Mr Fox where they should live, and he described to her his castle, and where it was; but, strange to say, did not ask her or her brothers to come and see it.

So one day, near the wedding-day, when her brothers were out, and Mı. Fox was away for a day or two on business, as he said, Lady Mary set out for Mr Fox's castle. And after many searchings, she came at last to it, and a fine strong house it was, with high walls and a deep moat. And when she came up to the gateway she saw written on it:

Be bold, be bold.

But as the gate was open, she went through it, and
59

found no one there. So she went up to the doorway, and over it she found written:

Be bold, be bold, but not too bold.

Still she went on, till she came into the hall, and went up the broad stairs till she came to a door in the gallery, over which was written:

Be bold, be bold, but not too bold,
Lest that your heart's blood should run cold.

But Lady Mary was a brave one, she was, and she opened the door, and what do you think she saw? Why, bodies and skeletons of beautiful young ladies all stained with blood. So Lady Mary thought it was high time to get out of that horrid place, and she closed the door, went through the gallery, and was just going down the stairs, and out of the hall, when who should she see through the window, but Mr Fox dragging a beautiful young lady along from the gateway to the door. Lady Mary rushed downstairs, and hid herself behind a cask just in time, as Mr Fox came in with the poor young lady who seemed to have fainted. Just as he got near Lady Mary, Mr Fox saw a diamond ring glittering on the finger of the young lady he was dragging, and he tried to pull it off. But it was tightly fixed, and would not come off, so Mr Fox cursed and swore, and drew his sword, raised it, and brought it down upon the hand of the poor lady. The sword cut off the hand, which jumped up into the air, and fell of all places in the world into Lady Mary's lap. Mr Fox looked about a bit, but did not think of looking behind the cask, so at last he went on dragging the young lady up the stairs into the Bloody Chamber.

As soon as she heard him pass through the gallery, Lady Mary crept out of the door, down through the gateway, and ran home as fast as she could.

Now it happened that the very next day the marriage contract of Lady Mary and Mr Fox was to be signed, and there was a splendid breakfast before that. And when Mr Fox was seated at the table opposite Lady Mary, he looked at her. 'How pale you are this morning, my dear.' 'Yes,' said she, 'I had a bad night's rest last night. I had horrible dreams.' 'Dreams go by contraries,' said Mr Fox; 'but tell us your dream, and your sweet voice will make the time pass till the happy hour comes.'

'I dreamed,' said Lady Mary, 'that I went yester-morn to your castle, and I found it in the woods, with high walls, and a deep moat, and over the gateway was written:

Be bold, be bold.'

'But it is not so, nor it was not so,' said Mr Fox. 'And when I came to the doorway over it was written:

Be bold, be bold, but not too bold.'

'It is not so, nor it was not so,' said Mr Fox.

61

'And then I went upstairs, and came to a gallery, at the end of which was a door on which was written:

Be bold, be bold, but not too bold,
Lest that your heart's blood should run cold.'

'It is not so, nor it was not so,' said Mr Fox.

'And then—and then I opened the door, and the room was filled with bodies and skeletons of poor dead women, all stained with their blood.'

'It is not so, nor it was not so. And God forbid it should be so,' said Mr Fox.

'I then dreamed that I rushed down the gallery, and just as I was going down the stairs, I saw you, Mr Fox, coming up to the hall door, dragging after you a poor young lady, rich and beautiful.'

'It is not so, nor it was not so. And God forbid it should be so,' said Mr Fox.

'I rushed downstairs, just in time to hide myself behind a cask, when you, Mr Fox, came in dragging the young lady by the arm. And, as you passed me, Mr Fox, I thought I saw you try to get off her diamond ring, and when you could not, Mr Fox, it seemed to me in my dream, that you out with your sword and hacked off the poor lady's hand to get the ring.'

'It is not so, nor was it so. And God forbid it should be so,' said Mr Fox, and was going to say something else as he rose from his seat, when Lady Mary cried out:

'But it is so, and it was so. Here's hand and ring I

have to show,' and pulled out the lady's hand from her dress, and pointed it straight at Mr Fox.

At once her brothers and friends drew their swords and cut Mr Fox into a thousand pieces.

HIS OWN NUMBER

By WILLIAM CROFT DICKINSON

'WHAT DO YOU GAIN by putting a man into space?' asked Johnson, somewhat aggressively. 'Instruments are far more efficient.'

'But,' protested Hamilton, our Professor of Mathematical Physics, 'an astronaut can make use of instruments which don't respond to remote control. Also, he can bring the right instruments into work at exactly the right time in flight.'

'Maybe so,' returned Johnson. 'But what if he gets excited? The advantage of the instrument is that it never gets excited. It has no emotions. Its response is purely automatic.'

'Can you be sure of that?' asked Munro, from his chair by the fire. And, by the way he spoke, we could sense that there was something behind his question.

'If it is in perfect order, why not?' persisted Johnson.

'I don't know,' Munro replied, slowly. 'But I can tell you a tale of an electronic computer that was in perfect order and yet three times gave the same answer to an unfortunate technician.'

'Something like a wrist-watch which is affected by the pulse-beat of the wearer?' suggested Hayles.

'Something more than that,' said Munro. 'A great deal more. But what that "something" was, I simply don't know. Or can an instrument have "second sight", or respond to forces that are beyond our reckoning? I wish I knew the answer to that. However, I'll tell you my tale, and then each of you can try to explain it to his own satisfaction.'

As you probably know, when I first came here I came to a Research Fellowship in the Department of Mathematics. And, as it happened, one of the problems upon which I was engaged necessitated the use of an electronic computer. There were several in the Department, but the one which I normally used was quite a simple instrument: little more than an advanced calculator. I could 'programme' a number of calculations, feed them into it, and, in less than a minute, out would come the answer which it would have taken me perhaps a month to work out by myself. Just that, and no more. And I wish I could say it was always: 'Just that, and no more.' For here comes my tale.

One afternoon, being somewhat rushed—for I had been invited to a sherry party in the Senate Room— I asked one of the technicians if he'd feed my calculations into the computer, and leave the result on my desk. By pure chance the man I asked to do the job for me was called Murdoch Finlayson: a Highlander from somewhere up in Wester Ross. He was a good fellow in every way, and as honest and conscientious as they make them. I say 'by pure chance'; but perhaps it was all foreordained that I should pick on Finlayson. Certainly it seemed so, in the end. But, at the time, all I wanted to do was to get away to a sherry party; Finlayson happened to be near at hand; and I knew that I could trust him.

I thought, when I asked him to do the job, and when I indicated the computer I wanted him to use, that he looked strangely hesitant, and even backed away a bit. I remember wondering if he had been wanting to leave early, and here was I keeping him tied to his work. But, just when I was about to say that there was no real hurry, and that I'd attend to it myself in the morning, he seemed to pull himself together, reached out for my calculations, and, with an odd look in his eyes, murmured something that sounded like 'the third time'.

I was a little puzzled by his reaction to what I thought was a simple request, and even more puzzled by that murmured remark about 'the third time'; but, being in a hurry, gave the matter no second thought and dashed off.

My sherry party lasted somewhat longer than I had expected and, when I returned to the Department, I found it deserted. Everyone had gone home. I walked over to my desk, and then stood there, dumbfounded. Instead of the somewhat complex formula I had expected, I saw one of the computer's sheets bearing a simple number. A simple line of six digits. I won't give you the exact number on that sheet, but it was something like

585244

and underneath the number was a short note:

I recognized Finlayson's handwriting. But what did he mean by that cryptic statement? First of all, he had murmured something about 'the third time'; and now he had left a message saying: 'It's come for the third time.' And what was that simple line of digits, anyway? If it was supposed to be the answer to my series of calculations, it was no answer at all.

At first I felt slightly angry. What was Finlayson playing at? Then a vague feeling of uneasiness supervened. Finlayson was too sound and solid to be playing tricks with me. I remembered his hesitancy, and a new thought struck me: had it perhaps been fear? What could that number mean? As a line of digits, a six-figure number, I could see nothing unusual about it. It was a simple number, and nothing more. Then, for a time, I played with it. I cubed it; but I was no wiser. I added up the digits and cubed the total; I multiplied by three and tried again; and so forth and so on till I admitted that I was simply wasting my time. I could make nothing of it.

Unfortunately I didn't know where Finlayson lived, so perforce I had to contain my curiosity until the next morning. Also I had to contain that vague feeling of uneasiness which still persisted. But the next morning, as soon as I had entered the Department, I sought him out.

'This is an extraordinary result, Finlayson,' I said, holding out the computer sheet which he had left on my desk.

'Aye, sir.'

'But surely the computer must have gone completely haywire.'

'The computer's all right, sir. But yon's the result it gave me, and I'm no liking it at all.'

'The computer can't be right,' I persisted. 'And your note seems to say that this is the third time you've received this result from it. Do you really mean that on three separate occasions, whatever the calculations you have put into this computer, it has each time returned this same number—585244?'

'It has that, sir. And it's unchancy. I'm no liking a machine that gives me yon same number three times. I'm thinking that maybe it's my own number. And now I'm afeared o' it. I'm for handing in my papers and leaving, sir. I'll away to my brother's to help with the sheep. 'Tis safer feeding a flock of ewes than tending a machine that aye gives you a queer number.'

'Nonsense,' I retorted. 'There's something wrong with the computer, or with the way in which you set it and fed in the calculations.'

'Maybe aye and maybe no, sir. But maybe I've been given my own number, and I'm no liking it at all. I'm wanting to leave.'

I realized that I was up against some form of Highland superstition. Finlayson had been given a simple number three times, and that was enough for him. Maybe it was 'his own number'—whatever that might mean. I realized, too, that he had made up his mind to go, and that nothing I could say would dissuade him. Sheep were safer than electronic computers.

'All right,' I said to him, 'I'll speak to the Dean. And if it is any comfort to you, I won't ask you to operate that computer again.'

He thanked me for what he called my 'consideration', and went back to his work. I, in turn, went straight to the Dean.

'What an extraordinary business,' said the Dean, when I had recounted the circumstances to him. 'I wouldn't have believed it of Finlayson. I would have said he was far too intelligent to let anything like that upset him. There's surely something wrong with that computer. It's a very old instrument. Let's have a look at it.'

And, naturally, 'having a look at it' included feeding in the calculations which I had previously given to Finlayson. The computer quickly gave us the result. And it was a result far different from Finlayson's simple number, 585244. Although it would have taken me days to check it, the result was a complex formula like the one I had expected.

The Dean muttered something to himself and then turned to me. 'We'll try it again. I have some calculations of my own to which I know the answer.'

He went to his room, came back with his calculations and fed them into the machine. A few seconds later, out came the computer's sheet bearing the answer.

'Perfectly correct,' said the Dean, crisply. 'Finlayson must have been imagining things. Or else, for some unknown reason, he has three times fed a wrong programme into the computer. Even then, he couldn't get an answer like 585244.'

'I don't know,' I replied, slowly. 'He's too good a technician to make mistakes. And carelessness is no explanation. He's convinced he has received that six-figure number on the last three occasions on which he has used this machine. I'm beginning to think he did—though don't ask me why. But he's also convinced that there's some premonition in it. "His own number" has turned up three times. And "the third time" is a kind of final summons. Superstition if you like, but I'm beginning to feel for him. I think we should let him go.'

'Very well,' returned the Dean with a sigh of resignation. 'Have it your own way. I'll tell him he can leave at the end of the week. But you know as well as I do how difficult it is to get good technicians.'

We sought out Finlayson and the Dean told him that if he was determined to go he could be released at the end of the week. The man's eyes lit up at the news, and his relief was obvious.

'I'll away to my brother's,' he said, delightedly. 'He'll be glad of my help, and I'll be glad to be helping him. Not that I've been unhappy in my work here, sir. I would not be saying that. But I'm kind of feared to be staying. And if ye had not said I could go, I doubt I would have been going all the same. Though it would not be like me to be doing a thing like that.'

'Where does your brother live?' the Dean asked, quickly changing the conversation.

'In Glen Ogle, sir, on the road from Lochearnhead to Killin.'

'A beautiful stretch of country,' I put in. 'Do you

know, I'll drive you there on Saturday morning if you like. It will be a lovely run. Where shall I pick you up?'

He accepted my offer with alacrity, and gave me the address of his lodgings.

I did not tell him of the two tests of the computer which the Dean and I had carried out.

The Saturday morning was fine and clear. I called for him at the address he had given me, and found him waiting, with his possessions packed into a large grip.

Once we had passed through Stirling and had reached the foothills of the Highlands, the beauty of the country seized hold of me. Finlayson's desire to join his brother amid these brown and purples, golds, blues and greens, seemed the most sensible thing in all the world. The sun made the hills a glory; Ben Ledi and Ben Vorlich raised their heads in the distance; and, as we left Callander, the long-continuing Falls of Leny cascaded over their rocks by the side of the road. Finlayson's thrice-recurring number was surely a blessing and not a curse.

We had run through Lochearnhead and had entered Glen Ogle when, just as I was about to ask Finlayson for the whereabouts of his brother's farm, the car suddenly slowed down and stopped. I knew the tank was practically full, for I had just put in eight gallons at Callander. My first thought was carburettor-trouble, or possibly a blocked feed. I loosened the bonnet-catch, got out, raised the bonnet, and went through all the usual checks. But, to my annoyance, I could find nothing wrong. The tank was full; feed, pump and carburettor were all functioning properly. I gave myself a few minor shocks as I tested the electrical circuits. Nothing wrong there. Coil, battery, distributor, plugs, were all in order. I reached over to the fascia board and pressed the self-starter. The starter-motor whirred noisily in the stillness, but the engine did not respond. Once more I tested every connection and every part. Again I pressed the self-starter, and again with no effect. Thoroughly exasperated, I turned to Finlayson who had joined me in this exhaustive check and who was as puzzled as I was.

'Well, and what do we do now?' I asked.

'I'll walk the two-three miles to my brother's,' he said. 'He has the tractor, and can tow us to the farm. Then maybe we can find out what has gone wrong.'

'Excellent!' I agreed. 'Off you go.'

I sat down on the grass and I watched him striding away until he disappeared round a bend in the road. A little later I got up, closed the bonnet of the car, and took a road map from one of the door-pockets. Perhaps there was an alternative route for my way back.

I had barely opened the map and laid it out on top of the bonnet when a car came tearing round the bend ahead. As soon as the driver saw me, he pulled up with a screech of his brakes and jumped out.

'For God's sake come back with me,' he cried. 'I've killed a man, just up the road. He walked right into me.'

A car came tearing round the bend

For a moment the shock of his words stunned me, and I stood irresolute.

'Quick!' he continued. 'We'll take your car. It will save the time of reversing mine.'

Without further ado, he jumped into the driver's seat of my car, pressed the self-starter and impatiently signalled to me to get in beside him.

So Finlayson was dead. Somehow I knew it was Finlayson. Dead in Glen Ogle where sheep were safer than machines. He had walked from my useless car to meet his death round the bend in the road.

My useless car! With a sudden tremor of every nerve I realized that the engine was turning over as smoothly as it had ever done.

Had the whole world turned upside down?

Mechanically I got in and sat down beside the man. He drove a short distance round the bend and then slowly came to a halt. I saw at once that my fears were only too true. Finlayson was dead. The man had lifted him on to the grass that verged the road. I got out and bent over him. There was nothing I could do.

'I saw him walking on his own side of the road,' I heard the man saying to me. 'And I was on my own side too. But he couldn't have seen me or heard me. Just when I should have passed him, he suddenly crossed over. My God! He crossed right in front of me! Do you think he was deaf? Or perhaps he was thinking of something. Absent-minded. How else could he walk right into me?'

The man was talking on and on. Later, I realized he had to talk. It was the only relief for him. But I was not listening. Finlayson lay there, broken, still. Seeking life, he had found death. His 'number' had 'come up' three times. It was 'unchancy'. To hell with his number! What had that to do with this?

At the subsequent inquiry, the driver of the car was completely exonerated. In a moment of absent-mindedness Finlayson had stepped across the road right into the path of the oncoming car. The finding was clear and definite. Yet for me, I could not forget that the unhappy man had felt some premonition of mischance. He had decided to cheat mischance and seek safety amid the hills. And mischance and death had met him there. Yet what possible connection could there be between 'his number,' 585244, and his death?

At first I thought that Finlayson had possibly seen 'his number' on a telegraph pole, or perhaps on a pylon, and, startled, had crossed the road to look at it more clearly. I made a special journey to Lochearnhead, parked my car there, and examined every bit of the road from the place where my car had 'broken down' to the place were Finlayson had been killed. But I could find nothing to substantiate my theory.

And why had my car so mysteriously broken down and then so mysteriously started again? Could it be that the fates had decreed the time and place of the death of Murdoch Finlayson and had used the puny machines of man's invention for their decree's fulfilment? An electronic computer that could be made to give the one number, and an internal combustion engine that could be brought to a halt. And why that number? Why that number?

That one question so dominated my mind that it ruined my work by day and my rest by night. And then, perhaps a fortnight after Finlayson's death, I was given an answer; yet it was an answer that still left everything unexplained.

I had gone over to the Staff House for lunch, and had joined a table where, too late, I found an animated discussion in progress to the effect that members of the Faculty of Arts were too ignorant of elementary science, and members of the Faculty of Science too ignorant of the arts. I was in no mood to join in the discussion, though politeness demanded that occasionally I should put in my word. The table gradually emptied until only Crossland, the Professor of Geography, and I were left.

'Neither Science nor Arts can answer some of our questions,' I said to him, bitterly.

'I know,' he replied. 'It must have been a terrible shock for you. I suppose we shall never know why that computer returned the one number to Finlayson three times. That is, if it did. And what was the number, by the way? I never heard.'

'A simple line of six digits—585244.'

'Sounds just like a normal national grid reference,' Crossland commented.

'A normal national grid reference?' I queried.

'Yes. Surely you know our national grid system for map-references. Or,' he continued with a smile, 'is this a case of scientist knowing too little of the work in the Faculty of Arts?'

'You've scored a point there,' I replied. 'I'm afraid I'm completely ignorant of this grid system of yours.'

'Probably you've been using motoring-maps too much.' he conceded. 'But the grid is quite simple. If you look at any sheet of the Ordnance Survey you will see that it is divided into kilometre squares by grid lines, numbered from 0 to 99, running west to east, and 0 to 99, running south to north. Then, within each kilometre square, a closer definition is obtained by measuring in tenths between the grid lines. Thus a particular spot, say a farm-steading or a spinney, can be pin-pointed on the map, within its numbered square, by a grid-reference which runs to six figures: three, west to east; and three, south to north. A six-figure number, which is known as the "normal national grid reference".'

For a minute or so I digested this in silence.

'Can we go over to your map-room?' I asked.

'Surely,' he said, a little surprised. 'And see on a map how it works?'

'Yes.'

We went over to Crossland's department.

'Any particular map?' he asked.

'Yes. A map of Western Perthshire.'

Crossland produced the Ordnance Survey Sheet. I looked at it almost with reluctance.

Taking out a pencil, I pointed to the place on the map where, as near as I could judge, Finlayson had met his death. 'What would be the grid reference for that particular spot?' I asked, and wondered at the strangeness of my voice.

Crossland picked up a transparent slide and bent over the map. I heard him take in his breath. He straightened himself, and when he turned to look at me his eyes were troubled and questioning.

'Yes,' concluded Munro. 'I needn't tell you what the grid reference was. But can anyone tell me why Finlayson was given that number three times on an electronic computer? Or why my car "broke down", so that he could walk of his own accord to that very spot?'

THE MAN WHO WALKED WIDDERSHINS ROUND THE KIRK

By SORCHE NIC LEODHAS

WHEN YOU go round anything you want to be sure to go clockwise—that is, the way the hands of a clock travel, from right to left. That's what the Scots call 'going deasil'. If you go the other way, you're going backwards, from left to right, and that is called 'going widdershins', and it's a dangerous thing to do for it's bound to bring you bad luck.

There was once a young man who lived in a village t'other side of Galashiels who walked widdershins round a kirk, and a terrible experience he got from it. It wasn't because he didn't know any better. He'd heard his mother and his grandmother and other old folk talk about it many a time. The trouble with him was that he was one of the sort that is so stubborn and so set upon going their own gait that the only way to steer them is to tell them to go the other way. Then you can be sure they'll go the way you want them to go.

The name of this lad was Alistair MacGillivray, but everybody called him Sandy. One day Sandy and a friend of his were taking a short cut through the kirk-yard. They had to go round the kirk to reach the path they were going to take beyond it. When they got to the corner of the kirkyard near the building, Sandy turned to the right to go round it.

'Och, nay, Sandy!' his friend exclaimed, forgetting for a minute that Sandy wouldn't take a telling. 'You cannot go round the kirk that direction.'

'Why not, then?' asked Sandy.

'It's widdershins that way,' his friend protested.

'What of it?' Sandy said. 'It's shorter than going round the other way. Come along, lad!'

But his friend held back. 'I'd not have the dare, Sandy. It would just be asking for trouble, to walk widdershins. Especially round the kirk. You can't do it.'

'I can, indeed,' said Sandy, growing more stubborn every minute. 'And what's more, I will. I'll walk widdershins the whole way round just to show you. You watch me!'

So Sandy went off to the front of the church and made a sharp turn to the right side of it, whistling a tune like a lark to show he didn't care at all. He turned at the corner and went along the right side of the kirk. Then across the back he went and down the other side, going widdershins all the way.

When he turned the last corner and came back to the front of it, he found his friend standing there in the kirkyard waiting for him and looking awful scared.

'Well, then, I did it,' Sandy said triumphantly, starting to walk over to his friend. But just then he set his foot down right on the place he started out from and poof! He disappeared!

80

He was there one minute and the next minute he wasn't, just like a candle flame blown out by the wind.

His friend blinked and his jaw dropped and he stared at the empty space where Sandy had just been standing. Then he gave a great screech and turned about and raced off to the village to spread the news that something awful had happened to Sandy MacGillivray.

Sandy did not realise at all that anything strange had happened to him, though he did have a queer sort of feeling that he couldn't quite explain. His friend had behaved as if he had suddenly gone daft, and Sandy was terribly puzzled about it. He went over to the low wall that ran round the kirkyard and sat down on top of it to think things over and try to work out what had made his friend go off shrieking in such a daft way.

While he was sitting there and thinking, with his hands lying loose-like on his knees, Sandy happened to let his eyes fall upon them. He got a horrible fright. Losh! He had no hands! Nor any knees, nor any legs or feet! In fact, he had no body at all, as far as he could see. Then Sandy understood what had happened to him. *He'd turned into a ghost!* It all came from walking widdershins round the kirk.

The worst of it was that he wasn't even a proper ghost, with a corpse that had been waked by his friends and buried. He was a ghost without even a grave that he could call his own. Och, poor Sandy MacGillivray was in a sad, sad state.

Well, he was sitting there feeling sorry for himself

and wondering what he was to do about it, when he heard a lot of clamour from the road. A crowd of folk from the village came tearing up to the kirkyard with his friend at the head of them leading the way.

They all poured into the kirkyard and began looking about among the gravestones for Sandy, calling him by name. They didn't believe what Sandy's friend had told them about the way Sandy had vanished. All of them were sure that they'd be finding him hiding somewhere. 'Twas just the sort of faladha Sandy'd like to play on them, and him being always ready for a joke.

They paid no heed to Sandy, sitting on the kirkyard wall, which was not surprising, since they couldn't see him. After he'd called out to them a couple of times to tell them where to find him, he discovered that they couldn't hear him either. So he gave up trying and just sat there on the wall watching them hunting for him and feeling very low in his spirits.

When they had called and hunted for a long while without finding hide or hair of Sandy, they began to tell one another that maybe Sandy's friend was right, and Sandy had vanished after all. At any rate they were tired of hunting for him and they might as well go back to the village. For some reason or other they didn't feel comfortable in the kirkyard after what had happened to Sandy MacGillivray there.

They stood for a while talking about Sandy just outside the kirkyard. Sandy was so near to them he could have leaned out and touched them if he wanted.

He didn't bother because he thought they wouldn't feel his touch. He had to grin to think of the fright he could give them if they could. But then he heard his name spoken and began to listen to what was being said.

'I told him not to walk widdershins,' Sandy's friend lamented. 'I told him, but he wouldn't heed me.'

'And you the fool of the world to tell him that!' said one of the searchers. 'And you knowing Sandy the way you do.'

' 'Twas the worst thing you could do,' said another. 'Tell Sandy to do one thing and you might be sure he'd do the very opposite. Where were your wits, lad?'

'I wouldn't want to be saying a word against Sandy now that he's no longer with us—in a manner of speaking,' said another in a pious tone. But he spoiled it by adding. 'But I'll tell you this. I never saw a stubborner lad or one that was more contrary!'

It shocked Sandy quite a bit to hear how quick the others were to agree with the speaker. 'Och, aye!' 'Och, aye!' they said as they went down the road.

So there was poor Sandy MacGillivray, a ghost but not a proper ghost, left sitting all alone on the kirk-yard wall.

He'd never thought about himself before, or about what folk might think of him, but now he spent a long time turning what he'd heard about himself over in his mind. He had to admit that there was naught but truth in it. Stubborn he'd been and contrary he'd been, and he was in a terrible fix because of it.

What was he going to do now? He didn't like to go home because, ghost or not, he was sure his mother would know him, and it would give her a terrible fright. He wouldn't go to the village because folk would be gathered round talking about him, and like as not he wouldn't care at all for what they'd say. But he couldn't go on sitting here on the kirkyard wall, because after dark there might be other ghosts in the place, and Sandy was afraid of ghosts—proper ghosts, that is. What in the world was he going to do?

Then it came into his mind that since he'd got into trouble going round the kirk the wrong way, maybe going round it the right way would do him some good. Anyway, it was worth trying.

So he got down off the wall and went up to the front of the kirk and started off again. But this time he went the right way, from right to left, clockwise, going deasil all the way. He came slowly round the last corner and up to the front of the kirk, so scared that it wouldn't work that he could scarcely breathe. But the minute he set his foot on the place he'd started out from he felt a great shock that shook him from head to foot. He looked down at himself, and there he was again! Sandy MacGillivray, all his own self, flesh and blood and bones again.

Sandy patted his shoulders and his arms and his legs, and clapped his hands for joy. Och, 'twas a rare grand thing, so it was, to have a body back again.

When he got home his mother was setting food upon the table. She said to Sandy. 'The supper's ready. Will you have it, Sandy?' She was expecting

Sandy to say, 'Och, I'm not wanting it now.' Or else, 'Nay, I'll take my supper later,' Sandy always being so contrary.

But Sandy gave her the surprise of the world. He slipped into his own place across from his father. 'Aye,' said Sandy meekly, 'I'll have my supper now.'

While he was eating his supper up came his friend with a deputation of lads from the village. They all looked solemn and mournful for they'd come to tell Sandy's family that Sandy had disappeared. When they saw him sitting there they couldn't believe their eyes.

'Is it yourself, Sandy?' they all cried as they gathered round him.

'Aye,' said Sandy calmly. 'Who else would it be?'

Sandy's friend could never explain it. Sandy never said a word. Folks began to say that Sandy's friend had dreamed it all. He had to take so much of their joking about it that sometimes he wished that he had disappeared himself.

THE FLOWERING OF THE STRANGE ORCHID

By H. G. WELLS

THE buying of orchids always has in it a certain speculative flavour. You have before you the brown shrivelled limp of tissue, and for the rest you must trust your judgment, or the auctioneer, or your good luck, as your taste may incline. The plant may be moribund or dead, or it may be just a respectable purchase, fair value for your money, or perhaps— for the thing has happened again and again—there slowly unfolds before the delighted eyes of the happy purchaser, day after day, some new variety, some novel richness, a strange twist of labellum, or some subtler coloration or unexpected mimicry. Pride, beauty, and profit blossom together on one delicate green spike, and, it may be, even immortality. For the new miracle of nature may stand in need of a new specific name, and what so convenient as that of its discoverer? "Johnsmithia!" There have been worse names.

It was perhaps the hope of some such happy discovery that made Winter-Wedderburn such a frequent attendant at these sales—that hope, and also, maybe, the fact that he had nothing else of the slightest interest to do in the world. He was a shy, lonely, rather ineffectual man, provided with just enough income to keep off the spur of necessity, and not enough nervous energy to make him seek any exacting employments. He might have collected stamps or coins, or translated Horace, or bound books, or invented new species of diatoms. But as it happened, he grew orchids, and had one ambitious little hothouse.

"I have a fancy," he said over his coffee, "that something is going to happen to me to-day." He spoke—as he moved and thought—slowly.

"Oh, don't say *that!*" said his housekeeper—who was also his remote cousin. For "something happening" was a euphemism that meant only one thing to her.

"You misunderstand me. I mean nothing unpleasant . . . though what I do mean I scarcely know.

"To-day," he continued, after a pause, "Peters' are going to sell a batch of plants from the Andamans and the Indies. I shall go up and see what they have. It may be I shall buy something good unawares. That may be it."

He passed his cup for his second cupful of coffee.

"Are these the things collected by that poor young fellow you told me of the other day?" asked his cousin, as she filled his cup.

"Yes," he said, and became meditative over a piece of toast.

"Nothing ever does happen to me," he remarked presently, beginning to think aloud. "I wonder why?

Things enough happen to other people. There is Harvey. Only the other week; on Monday he picked up sixpence, on Wednesday his chicks all had the staggers, on Friday his cousin came home from Australia, and on Saturday he broke his ankle. What a whirl of excitement!—compared to me."

"I think I would rather be without so much excitement," said his housekeeper. "It can't be good for you."

"I suppose it's troublesome. Still . . . you see, nothing ever happens to me. When I was a little boy I never had accidents. I never fell in love as I grew up. Never married. . . . I wonder how it feels to have something happen to you, something really remarkable.

"That orchid-collector was only thirty-six—twenty years younger than myself—when he died. And he had been married twice and divorced once; he had had malarial fever four times, and once he broke his thigh. He killed a Malay once, and once he was wounded by a poisoned dart. And in the end he was killed by jungle leeches. It must have all been very troublesome, but then it must have been very interesting, you know—except, perhaps, the leeches."

"I am sure it was not good for him," said the lady with conviction.

"Perhaps not." And then Wedderburn looked at his watch. "Twenty-three minutes past eight. I am going up by the quarter to twelve train, so that there is plenty of time. I think I shall wear my alpaca jacket—it is quite warm enough—and my grey felt hat and brown shoes. I suppose——"

He glanced out of the window at the serene sky and sunlit garden, and then nervously at his cousin's face.

"I think you had better take an umbrella if you are going to London," she said in a voice that admitted of no denial. "There's all between here and the station coming back."

When he returned he was in a state of mild excitement. He had made a purchase. It was rare that he could make up his mind quickly enough to buy, but this time he had done so.

"There are Vandas," he said, "and a Dendrobe and some Palæonophis." He surveyed his purchases lovingly as he consumed his soup. They were laid out on the spotless tablecloth before him, and he was telling his cousin all about them as he slowly meandered through his dinner. It was his custom to live all his visits to London over again in the evening for her and his own entertainment.

"I knew something would happen to-day. And I have bought all these. Some of them—some of them —I feel sure, do you know, that some of them will be remarkable. I don't know how it is, but I feel just as sure as if someone had told me that some of these will turn out remarkable.

"That one"—he pointed to a shrivelled rhizome— "was not identified. It may be a Palæonophis—or it may not. It may be a new species, or even a new genus. And it was the last that poor Batten ever collected."

"I don't like the look of it," said his housekeeper. "It's such an ugly shape."

"To me it scarcely seems to have a shape."

"I don't like those things that stick out," said his housekeeper.

"It shall be put away in a pot to-morrow."

"It looks," said the housekeeper, "like a spider shamming dead."

Wedderburn smiled and surveyed the root with his head on one side. "It is certainly not a pretty lump of stuff. But you can never judge of these things from their dry appearance. It may turn out to be a very beautiful orchid indeed. How busy I shall be to-morrow! I must see to-night just exactly what to do with these things, and to-morrow, I shall set to work."

"They found poor Batten lying dead, or dying, in a mangrove swamp—I forget which," he began again presently, "with one of these very orchids crushed up under his body. He had been unwell for some days with some kind of native fever, and I suppose he fainted. These mangrove swamps are very unwholesome. Every drop of blood, they say, was taken out of him by the jungle-leeches. It may be that very plant that cost him his life to obtain."

"I think none the better of it for that."

"Men must work though women may weep," said Wedderburn with profound gravity.

"Fancy dying away from every comfort in a nasty swamp! Fancy being ill of fever with nothing to take but chlorodyne and quinine—if men were left to themselves they would live on chlorodyne and quinine—and no one round you but horrible natives! They say the Andaman islanders are most disgusting wretches—and, anyhow, they can scarcley make good nurses, not having the necessary training. And just for people in England to have orchids!"

"I don't suppose it was comfortable, but some men seem to enjoy that kind of thing," said Wedderburn. "Anyhow, the natives of his party were sufficiently civilised to take care of all his collection until his colleague, who was an ornithologist, came back again from the interior; though they could not tell the species of the orchid, and had let it wither. And it makes these things more interesting."

"It makes them disgusting. I should be afraid of some of the malaria clinging to them. And just think, there has been a dead body lying across that ugly thing! I never thought of that before. There! I declare I cannot eat another mouthful of dinner."

"I will take them off the table if you like, and put them in the window-seat. I can see them just as well there."

The next few days he was indeed singularly busy in his steamy little hothouse, fussing about with charcoal, lumps of teak, moss, and all the other mysteries of the orchid cultivator. He considered he was having a wonderfully eventful time. In the evening he would talk about these new orchids to his friends, and over and over again he reverted to his expectation of something strange.

Several of the Vandas and the Dendrobium died under his care, but presently the strange orchid began to show signs of life. He was delighted, and took his housekeeper right away from jam-making to see it at once, directly he made the discovery.

"That is a bud," he said, "and presently there will be a lot of leaves there, and those little things coming out here are aerial rootlets."

"They look to me like little white fingers poking out of the brown," said his housekeeper. "I don't like them."

"Why not?"

"I don't know. They look like fingers trying to get at you. I can't help my likes and dislikes."

"I don't know for certain, but I don't *think* there are any orchids I know that have aerial rootlets quite like that. It may be my fancy, of course. You see they are a little flattened at the ends."

"I don't like 'em," said his housekeeper, suddenly shivering and turning away. "I know it's very silly of me—and I'm very sorry, particularly as you like the things so much. But I can't help thinking of that corpse."

"But it may not be that particular plant. That was merely a guess of mine."

His housekeeper shrugged her shoulders. "Anyhow, I don't like it," she said.

Wedderburn felt a little hurt at her dislike to the plant.

But that did not prevent his talking to her about orchids generally, and this orchid in particular, whenever he felt inclined.

"There are such queer things about orchids," he said one day; "such possibilities of surprises. You know, Darwin studied their fertilisation and showed that the whole structure of an ordinary orchid flower was contrived in order that moths might carry the pollen from plant to plant. Well, it seems that there are lots of orchids known, the flower of which cannot possibly be used for fertilisation in that way. Some of the Cypripediums, for instance; there are no insects known that can possibly fertilise them, and some of them have never been found with seed."

"But how do they form new plants?"

"By runners and tubers, and that kind of outgrowth. That is easily explained. The puzzle is, what are the flowers for?

"Very likely," he added, "*my* orchids may be something extraordinary in that way. If so I shall study it. I have often thought of making researches as Darwin did. But hitherto I have not found the time, or something else has happened to prevent it. The leaves are beginning to unfold now. I do wish you would come and see them!"

But she said that the orchid-house was so hot it gave her the headache. She had seen the plant once again, and the aerial rootlets, which were now some of them more than a foot long, had unfortunately reminded her of tentacles reaching out after something; and they got into her dreams, growing after her with incredible rapidity. So that she had settled to her entire satisfaction that she would not see that plant again, and Wedderburn had to admire its leaves alone. They were of the ordinary broad form, and a deep glossy green, with splashes and dots of deep red towards the base. He knew of no other leaves quite like them. The plant was placed on a low bench near the thermometer, and close by was a simple arrangement by which a tap dripped on

93

the hot-water pipes and kept the air steamy. And he spent his afternoons now with some regularity meditating on the approaching flowering of this strange plant.

And at last the great thing happened. Directly he entered the little glass house he knew that the spike had burst out, although his great *Palæonophis Lowii* hid the corner where his new darling stood. There was a new odour in the air, a rich, intensely sweet scent, that overpowered every other in that crowded, steaming little greenhouse.

Directly he noticed this he hurried down to the strange orchid. And, behold! the trailing green spikes bore now three great splashes of blossom, from which this overpowering sweetness proceeded. He stopped before them in an ecstasy of admiration.

The flowers where white, with streaks of golden orange upon the petals; the heavy labellum was coiled into an intricate projection, and a wonderful bluish purple mingled there with the gold. He could see at once that the genus was altogether a new one. And the insufferable scent! How hot the place was! The blossoms swam before his eyes.

He would see if the temperature was right. He made a step towards the thermometer. Suddenly everything appeared unsteady. The bricks on the floor were dancing up and down. Then the white blossoms, the green leaves behind them, the whole greenhouse, seemed to sweep sideways, and then in a curve upward.

* * *

At half-past four his cousin made the tea, accord-

The whole greenhouse seemed to sweep sideways

ing to their invariable custom. But Wedderburn did not come in for his tea.

"He is worshipping that horrid orchid," she told herself, and waited ten minutes. "His watch must have stopped. I will go and call him."

She went straight to the hothouse, and, opening the door, called his name. There was no reply. She noticed that the air was very close, and loaded with an intense perfume. Then she saw something lying on the bricks between the hot-water pipes.

For a minute, perhaps, she stood motionless.

He was lying, face upward, at the foot of the strange orchid. The tentacle-like aerial rootlets no longer swayed freely in the air, but were crowded together, a tangle of grey ropes, and stretched tight, with their ends closely applied to his chin and neck and hands. She did not understand. Then she saw from under one of the exultant tentacles upon his cheek there trickled a little thread of blood.

With an inarticulate cry she ran towards him, and tried to pull him away from the leech-like suckers. She snapped two of these tentacles, and their sap dripped red.

Then the overpowering scent of the blossom began to make her head reel. How they clung to him! She tore at the tough ropes, and he and the white inflorescence swam about her. She felt she was fainting, knew she must not. She left him and hastily opened the nearest door, and, after she had panted for a moment in the fresh air, she had a brilliant inspiration. She caught up a flower-pot and smashed in the windows at the end of the greenhouse. Then she re-entered. She tugged now with renewed strength at Wedderburn's motionless body, and brought the strange orchid crashing to the floor. It still clung with the grimmest tenacity to its victim. In a frenzy, she lugged it and him into the open air.

Then she thought of tearing through the sucker rootlets one by one, and in another minute she had released him and was dragging him away from the horror.

He was white and bleeding from a dozen circular patches.

The odd-job man was coming up the garden, amazed at the smashing of glass, and saw her emerge, hauling the inanimate body with red-stained hands. For a moment he thought impossible things.

"Bring some water!" she cried, and her voice dispelled his fancies. When, with unnatural alacrity, he returned with the water, he found her weeping with excitement, and with Wedderburn's head upon her knee, wiping blood from his face.

"What's the matter?" said Wedderburn, opening his eyes feebly, and closing them again at once.

"Go and tell Annie to come out here to me, and then go for Dr. Haddon at once," she said to the odd-job man as soon as he brought the water; and added, seeing he hesitated, "I will tell you all about it when you come back."

Presently Wedderburn opened his eyes again, and, seeing that he was troubled by the puzzle of his position, she explained to him, "You fainted in the hothouse."

"And the orchid?"

D

"I will see to that," she said.

Wedderburn had lost a good deal of blood, but beyond that he had suffered no very great injury. They gave him brandy mixed with some pink extract of meat, and carried him upstairs to bed. His housekeeper told her incredible story in fragments to Dr. Haddon. "Come to the orchid-house and see," she said.

The cold outer air was blowing in through the open door, and the sickly perfume was almost dispelled. Most of the torn aerial rootlets lay already withered amidst a number of dark stains upon the bricks. The stem of the inflorescence was broken by the fall of the plant, and the flowers were growing limp and brown at the edges of the petals. The doctor stooped towards it, then saw that one of the aerial rootlets still stirred feebly, and hesitated.

The next morning the strange orchid still lay there, black now and putrescent. The door banged intermittently in the morning breeze, and all the array of Wedderburn's orchids was shrivelled and prostrate. But Wedderburn himself was bright and garrulous upstairs in the glory of his strange adventure.

THE UGLY—WUGLIES

By EDITH NESBIT

Gerald, Kathleen and Jimmy have to 'holiday' in the unfriendly atmosphere of an empty boarding school. But things brighten up when their friend Mabel finds a wish-granting ring, hidden in the castle nearby, where she lives with her Aunt, the housekeeper. So far, this ring has only made them rather inconveniently invisible! But the magic wears off after twenty-four hours, and now the four children are enjoying normal life again—magic forgotten—in the excitement of putting on a play for Mademoiselle, the pretty French mistress who is looking after them, and Eliza, the maid . . .

IT WAS still good daylight when the dinner-bell rang —the signal had been agreed upon at tea-time, and carefully explained to Eliza. Mademoiselle laid down her book and passed out of the sunset-yellow-ed hall into the faint yellow gaslight of the dining-room. The giggling Eliza held the door open before her, and followed her in. The shutters had been closed—streaks of daylight showed above and below

99

them. The green-and-black tablecloths of the school dining-tables were supported on the clothes-line from the backyard. The line sagged in a graceful curve, but it answered its purpose of supporting the curtains which concealed that part of the room which was the stage.

Rows of chairs had been placed across the other end of the room—all the chairs in the house, as it seemed—and Mademoiselle started violently when she saw that fully half a dozen of these chairs were occupied. And by the queerest people, too—an old woman with a poke bonnet tied under her chin with a red handkerchief, a lady in a large straw hat wreathed in flowers and the oddest hands that stuck out over the chair in front of her, several men with strange, clumsy figures, and all with hats on.

"But," whispered Mademoiselle, through the chinks of the tablecloths, "you have then invited other friends? You should have asked me, my children."

Laughter and something like a "hurrah" answered her from behind the folds of the curtaining table-cloths.

"All right, Mademoiselle," cried Mabel; "turn the gas up. It's only part of the entertainment."

Eliza, still giggling, pushed through the lines of chairs, knocking off the hat of one of the visitors as she did so, and turned up the three incandescent burners.

Mademoiselle looked at the figure seated nearest to her, stooped to look more closely, half laughed, quite screamed, and sat down suddenly.

100

"Oh!" she cried, "they are not alive!"

Eliza, with a much louder scream, had found out the same thing and announced it differently. "They ain't got no insides," said she. The seven members of the audience seated among the wilderness of chairs had, indeed, no insides to speak of. Their bodies were bolsters and rolled-up blankets; their spines were broom-handles, and their arm and leg bones were hockey sticks and umbrellas. Their shoulders were the wooden cross-pieces that Mademoiselle used for keeping her jackets in shape; their hands were gloves stuffed out with handkerchiefs; and their faces were the paper masks painted in the afternoon by the un-tutored brush of Gerald, tied on to the round heads made of the ends of stuffed bolster-cases. The faces were really rather dreadful. Gerald had done his best, but even after his best had been done you would hardly have known they were faces, some of them, if they hadn't been in the positions which faces usually occupy, between the collar and the hat. Their eyebrows were furious with lamp-black frowns—their eyes the size, and almost the shape, of five-shilling pieces, and on their lips and cheeks had been spent much crimson lake and nearly the whole of a half-pan of vermilion.

"You have made yourself an auditors, yes? Bravo!" cried Mademoiselle, recovering herself and beginning to clap. And to the sound of that clapping the curtain went up—or, rather, apart. A voice said, in a breathless, choked way, "Beauty and the Beast," and the stage was revealed.

It was a real stage too—the dining-tables pushed

close together and covered with pink-and-white counterpanes. It was a little unsteady and creaky to walk on, but very imposing to look at. The scene was simple, but convincing. A big sheet of cardboard, bent square, with slits cut in it and a candle behind, represented, the domestic hearth; a round hat-tin of Eliza's, supported on a stool with a nightlight under it, could not have been mistaken, save by wilful malice, for anying but a copper. A wastepaper basket with two or three school dusters and an overcoat in it, and a pair of blue pyjamas over the back of a chair, put the finishing touch to the scene. It did not need the announcement from the wings, "The laundry at Beauty's home." It was so plainly a laundry and nothing else.

In the wings: "They look just like a real audience, don't they?" whispered Mabel. "Go on, Jimmy,—don't forget the Merchant has to be pompous and use long words."

Jimmy, enlarged by pillows under Gerald's best overcoat, which had been intentionally bought with a view to his probable growth during the two years which it was intended to last him, a Turkish towel turban on his head and an open umbrella over it, opened the first act in a simple and swift soliloquy:

"I am the most unlucky merchant that ever was. I was once the richest merchant in Bagdad, but I lost all my ships, and now I live in a poor house that is all to bits; you can see how the rain comes through the roof, and my daughters take in washing. And——"

The pause might have seemed long, but Gerald

rustled in, elegant in Mademoiselle's pink dressing-gown and the character of the eldest daughter.

"A nice drying day," he minced. "Pa dear, put the umbrella the other way up. It'll save us going out in the rain to fetch water. Come on, sisters, dear father's got us a new wash-tub. Here's luxury!"

Round the umbrella, now held the wrong way up, the three sisters knelt and washed imaginary linen. Kathleen wore a violet skirt of Eliza's, a blue blouse of her own, and a cap of knotted handkerchiefs. A white nightdress girt with a white apron and two red carnations in Mabel's black hair left no doubt as to which of the three was Beauty.

The scene went very well. The final dance with waving towels was all that there is of charming, Mademoiselle said; and Eliza was so much amused that, as she said, she got quite a nasty stitch along of laughing so hearty.

You know pretty well what Beauty and the Beast would be like acted by four children who had spent the afternoon in arranging their costumes and so had left no time for rehearsing what they had to say. Yet it delighted them, and it charmed their audience. And what more can any play do, even Shakespeare's? Mabel, in her Princess clothes, was a resplendent Beauty; and Gerald a Beast who wore the drawing-room hearthrugs with an air of indescribable distinction. If Jimmy was not a talkative merchant, he made it up with a stoutness practically unlimited, and Kathleen surprised and delighted even herself by the quickness with which she changed from one to the other of the minor characters—fairies, servants, and messengers. It was at the end of the second act that Mabel, whose costume, having reached the height of elegance, could not be bettered and therefore did not need to be changed, said to Gerald, sweltering under the weighty magnificence of his beast-skin:—

"I say, you might let us have the ring back."

"I'm going to," said Gerald, who had quite forgotten it. "I'll give it you in the next scene. Only don't lose it, or go putting it on. You might go out all together and never be seen again, or you might get seven times as visible as any one else, so that all the rest of us would look like shadows beside you, you'd be so thick, or——"

"Ready!" said Kathleen, bustling in, once more a wicked sister.

Gerald managed to get his hand into his pocket under his hearthrug, and when he rolled his eyes in agonies of sentiment, and said, "Farewell, dear Beauty! Return quickly, for if you remain long absent from your faithful beast he will assuredly perish," he pressed a ring into her hand and added: "This is a magic ring that will give you anything you wish. When you desire to return to your own disinterested beast, put on the ring and utter your wish. Instantly you will be by my side."

Beauty-Mabel took the ring, and it was *the* ring.

The curtains closed to warm applause from two pairs of hands.

The next scene went splendidly. The sisters were almost *too* natural in their disagreeableness, and Beauty's annoyance when they splashed her Princess's dress with real soap and water was considered a miracle of good acting. Even the merchant rose to something more than mere pillows, and the curtain fell on his pathetic assurance that in the absence of his dear Beauty he was wasting away to a shadow. And again two pairs of hands applauded.

"Here, Mabel, catch hold," Gerald appealed from under the weight of a towel-horse, the tea-urn, the tea-tray, and the green baize apron of the boot boy, which together with four red geraniums from the landing, the pampas-grass from the drawing-room fireplace, and the india-rubber plants from the drawing-room window were to represent the fountains and garden of the last act. The applause had died away.

"I wish," said Mabel, taking on herself the weight of the tea-urn, "I wish those creatures we made were alive. We should get something like applause then."

"I'm jolly glad they aren't," said Gerald, arranging the baize and the towel-horse, "Brutes! It makes me feel quite silly when I catch their paper eyes."

The curtains were drawn back. There lay the hearth-rug-coated beast, in flat abandonment among the tropic beauties of the garden, the pampas-grass shrubbery, the india-rubber plant bushes, the geranium-trees and the urn fountain. Beauty was ready to make her great entry in all the thrilling splendour of despair. And then suddenly it all happened.

Mademoiselle began it: she applauded the garden scene—with hurried little clappings of her quick French hands. Eliza's fat red palms followed heavily, and then—some one else was clapping, six or seven people, and their clapping made a dull padded sound. Nine faces instead of two were turned towards the stage, and seven out of the nine were painted, pointed paper faces. And every hand and every face was alive. The applause grew louder as Mabel glided forward, and as she paused and looked at the audience her unstudied pose of horror and amazement drew forth applause louder still; but it was not loud enough to drown the shrieks of Mademoiselle and Eliza as they rushed from the room; knocking chairs over and crushing each other in the doorway. Two distant doors banged, Mademoiselle's door and Eliza's door.

"Curtain! Curtain! Quick!" cried Beauty-Mabel, in a voice that wasn't Mabel's or the Beauty's. "Jerry—those things *have* come alive. Oh, whatever *shall* we do?"

Gerald in his hearthrugs leaped to his feet. Again that flat padded applause marked the swish of cloths on clothes-line as Jimmy and Kathleen drew the curtains.

"What's up?" they asked as they drew.

"You've done it this time!" said Gerald to the pink, perspiring Mabel. "Oh, bother these strings!"

"Can't you burst them? *I've* done it?" retorted Mabel. "I like that!"

"More than I do," said Gerald.

"Oh, it's all right," said Mabel. "Come on. We must go and pull the things to pieces—then they *can't* go on being alive."

"It's your fault, anyhow," said Gerald with every possible absence of gallantry. "Don't you see? It's turned into a wishing ring. I *knew* something different was going to happen. Get my knife out of my

106

pocket—this string's in a knot. Jimmy, Cathy, those Ugly-Wuglies have come alive—because Mabel wished it. Go out and pull them to pieces."

Jimmy and Cathy peeped through the curtain and recoiled with white faces and staring eyes. "Not me!" was the brief rejoinder of Jimmy. Cathy said, "Not much!" And she meant it, and one could see that.

And now, as Gerald, almost free of the hearth-rugs, broke his thumb-nail on the stiffest blade of his knife, a thick rustling and a sharp, heavy stumping sounded beyond the curtain.

"They're going out!" screamed Kathleen—"*walking* out—on their umbrella and broomstick legs. You can't stop them, Jerry, they're too awful!"

"Everybody in the town'll be insane by to-morrow night if we *don't* stop them," cried Gerald. "Here, give me the ring—I'll unwish them."

He caught the ring from the unresisting Mabel, cried, "I wish the Uglies *weren't* alive," and tore through the door. He saw, in fancy, Mabel's wish undone, and the empty hall strewed with limp bolsters, hats, umbrellas, coats and gloves, prone abject properties from which the brief life had gone out for ever. But the hall was crowded with live things, strange things—all horribly short as broomsticks and umbrellas are short. A limp hand gesticulated. A pointed white face with red cheeks looked up at him, and wide red lips said something, he could not tell what. The voice reminded him of the old beggar down by the bridge who had no roof to his mouth. These creatures had no roofs to their mouths, of course—they had no——

"Aa oo ré o me me oo a oo ho-el?" said the voice

107

The grisly band trooped out of the yard door

again. And it had said it four times before Gerald could collect himself sufficiently to understand that this horror—alive, and most likely quite uncontrollable—was saying, with a dreadful calm, polite persistence—

"Can you recommend me to a good hotel?"

*   *   *

The speaker had no inside to his head. Gerald had the best of reasons for knowing it. The speaker's coat had no shoulders inside it—only the cross-bar that a jacket is slung on by careful ladies. The hand raised in interrogation was not a hand at all; it was a glove lumpily stuffed with a pocket-handkerchiefs; and the arm attached to it was only Kathleen's school umbrella. Yet the whole thing was alive, and was asking a definite, and for anybody else, anybody who really *was* a body, a reasonable question.

With a sensation of inward sinking, Gerald realised that now or never was the time for him to rise to the occasion. And at the thought he inwardly sank more deeply than before. It seemed impossible to rise in the very smallest degree.

"I beg your pardon" was absolutely the best he could do; and the painted, pointed paper face turned to him once more, and once more said:—

"Aa oo ré o me me oo a oo ho-el?"

"You want a hotel?" Gerald repeated stupidly, "a *good* hotel?"

"A oo ho-el," reiterated the painted lips.

"I'm awfully sorry," Gerald went on—one can always be polite, of course, whatever happens, and politeness came natural to him—"but all our hotels shut so early—about eight, I think."

"Och em er," said the Ugly-Wugly. Gerald even now does not understand how that practical joke—hastily wrought of hat, overcoat, paper face and limp hands—could have managed, by just being alive, to become perfectly respectable, apparently about fifty years old, and obviously well off, known and respected in his own suburb—the kind of man who travels first class and smokes expensive cigars. Gerald knew this time, without need of repetition, that the Ugly-Wugly had said:—

"Knock 'em up."

"You can't," Gerald explained; "they're all stone deaf—every single person who keeps a hotel in this town. It's—" he wildly plunged—"it's a County Council law. Only deaf people allowed to keep hotels. It's because of the hops in the beer," he found himself adding; "you know, hops are so good for earache."

"I o wy ollo oo," said the respectable Ugly-Wugly; and Gerald was not surprised to find that the thing did "not quite follow him."

"It *is* a little difficult at first," he said. The other Ugly-Wuglies were crowding round. The lady in the poke bonnet said—Gerald found he was getting quite clever at understanding the conversation of those who had no roofs to their mouths:—

"If not a hotel, a lodging."

"My lodging is on the cold ground," sang itself unbidden and unavailing in Gerald's ear. Yet stay—was it unavailing?

"I do know a lodging," he said slowly, "but——"
The tallest of the Ugly-Wuglies pushed forward. He

110

was dressed in the old brown overcoat and top-hat which always hung on the school hat-stand to discourage possible burglars by deluding them into the idea that there was a gentleman-of-the-house, and that he was at home. He had an air at once more sporting and less reserved than that of the first speaker, and any one could see that he was not quite a gentleman.

"Wa I wo oo oh," he began, but the lady Ugly- Wugly in the flower-wreathed hat interrupted him. She spoke more distinctly than the others, owing, as Gerald found afterwards, to the fact that her mouth had been drawn *open,* and the flap cut from the aperture had been folded back—so that she really had something like a roof to her mouth, though it was only a paper one.

"What *I* want to know," Gerald understood her to say, "is where are the carriages we ordered?"

"I don't know," said Gerald, "but I'll find out. But we ought to be moving," he added; "you see, the performance is over, and they want to shut up the house and put the lights out. Let's be moving."

"Eh—ech e oo-ig," repeated the respectable Ugly-Wugly, and stepped towards the front door.

"Oo um oo," said the flower-wreathed one; her vermilion lips stretched in a smile.

"I shall be delighted," said Gerald with earnest courtesy, "to do anything, of course. Things do happen so awkwardly when you least expect it. I could go with you, and get you a lodging, if you'd only wait a few moments in the—in the yard. It's quite a superior sort of yard," he went on, as a wave of surprised disdain passed over their white paper faces—"not a common yard, you know; the pump," he added madly, "has just been painted green all over, and the dustbin is enamelled iron."

The Ugly-Wuglies turned to each other in consultation, and Gerald gathered that the greenness of the pump and the enamelled character of the dustbin made, in their opinion, all the difference.

"I'm awfully sorry," he urged eagerly, "to have to ask you to wait, but you see I've got an uncle who's quite mad, and I have to give him his gruel at half-past nine. He won't feed out of any hand but mind." Gerald did not mind what he said. The only people one is allowed to tell lies to are the Ugly-Wuglies; they are all clothes and have no insides, because they are not human beings, but only a sort of very real vision, and therefore cannot be really deceived, though they may seem to be.

Through the back door, down the iron steps into the yard, Gerald led the way, and the Ugly-Wuglies trooped after him. Some of them had boots, but the ones whose feet were only broomsticks or umbrellas found the open-work iron stairs very awkward.

"If you wouldn't *mind*," said Gerald, "just waiting *under* the balcony? My uncle is so *very* mad. If he were to see—see any strangers—I mean, even aristocratic ones—I couldn't answer for the consequences."

"Perhaps," said the flower-hatted lady nervously, "it would be better for us to try and find a lodging ourselves?"

"I wouldn't advise you to," said Gerald as grimly as he knew how; "the police here arrest *all* strangers. It's the new law the Liberals have just made," he added convincingly, "and you'd get the sort of lodging you wouldn't care for—I couldn't bear to think of you in a prison dungeon," he added tenderly.

"I ah wi oo er papers," said the respectable Ugly-Wugly, and added something that sounded like "disgraceful state of things."

However, they ranged themselves under the iron balcony. Gerald gave one last look at them and wondered, in his secret heart, why he was not frightened, though in his outside mind he was congratulating himself on his bravery. For the thing did look rather horrid. As he went up the steps he heard them talking among themselves—in that strange language of theirs, all oo's and ah's; and he thought he distinguished the voice of the respectable Ugly-Wugly saying, "Most gentlemanly lad," and the wreathed-hatted lady answering warmly: "Yes, indeed."

The coloured-glass door closed behind him. Behind him was the yard, peopled by seven impossible creatures. Before him lay the silent house, peopled, as he knew very well, by five human beings as frightened as human beings could be. You think, perhaps, that Ugly-Wuglies are nothing to be frightened of. That's only because you have never seen one come alive.

Of course the reason why Gerald was not afraid was that he had the ring; and, as you have seen, the wearer of that is not frightened by *anything* unless he touches that thing. But Gerald knew well enough how the others must be feeling. That was why he stopped for a moment in the hall to try and imagine what would have been most soothing to him if he had been as terrified as he knew they were.

"Cathy! I say! What ho, Jimmy! Mabel ahoy!" he cried in a loud, cheerful voice that sounded very unreal to himself.

The dining-room door opened a cautious inch.

"I say—such larks!" Gerald went on, shoving gently at the door with his shoulder. "Look out! what are you keeping the door shut for?"

"Are you—alone?" asked Kathleen in hushed, breathless tones.

"Yes, of course. Don't be a duffer!"

The door opened, revealing three scared faces and the disarranged chairs where that odd audience had sat.

"Where are they? Have you unwished them? We heard them talking. Horrible!"

"They're in the yard," said Gerald with the best imitation of joyous excitement that he could manage. "It *is* such fun!" They're just like real people, quite kind and jolly. It's the most ripping lark. Don't let on to Mademoiselle and Eliza. I'll square *them*. Then Kathleen and Jimmy must go to bed, and I'll see Mabel home, and as soon as we get outside I must find some sort of lodging for the Ugly-Wuglies—they *are* such fun though. I *do* wish you could all go with me."

"Fun?" echoed Kathleen dismally and doubting.

"Perfectly killing," Gerald asserted resolutely. "Now, you just listen to what I say to Mademoiselle and Eliza, and back me up for all you're worth."

"But," said Mabel, "you can't mean that you're going to leave me alone directly we get out, and go off with those horrible creatures. They look like fiends."

"You wait till you've seen them close," Gerald ad-

114

vised. "Why, they're just *ordinary*—the first thing one of them did was to ask me to recommend it to a good hotel! I couldn't understand it at first, because it has no roof to its mouth, of course."

It was a mistake to say that, Gerald knew it at once.

Mabel and Kathleen were holding hands in a way that plainly showed how a few moments ago they had been clinging to each other in an agony of terror. Now they clung again. And Jimmy, who was sitting on the edge of what had been the stage, kicking his boots against the pink counterpane, shuddered visibly.

"It doesn't *matter*," Gerald explained— "about the roofs, I mean; you soon get to understand. I heard them say I was a gentlemanly lad as I was coming away. They wouldn't have cared to notice a little thing like that if they'd been fiends, you know."

"It doesn't matter how gentlemanly they think you; if you don't see me home you *aren't*, that's all. Are you going to?" Mabel demanded.

"Of course I am. We shall have no end of a lark. Now for Mademoiselle."

He had put on his coat as he spoke and now ran up the stairs. The others, herding in the hall, could hear his light-hearted there's-nothing-unusual-the-matter-whatever-did-you-bolt-like-that-for knock at Mademoiselle's door, the reassuring "It's only me—Gerald, you know," the pause, the opening of the door, and the low-voiced parley that followed; then Mademoiselle and Gerald at Eliza's door, voices of reassurance; Eliza's terror, bluntly voluble, tactfully soothed.

"Wonder what lies he's telling them," Jimmy grumbled.

"Oh! not *lies*," said Mabel; "he's only telling them as much of the truth as it's good for them to know."

"If you'd been a man," said Jimmy witheringly, "you'd have been a beastly Jesuit, and hid up chimneys."

"If I were only just a boy," Mabel retorted, "I shouldn't be scared out of my life by a pack of old coats."

"I'm *so* sorry you were frightened," Gerald's honeyed tones floated down the staircase; "we didn't think about you being frightened. And it *was* a good trick, wasn't it?"

"There!" whispered Jimmy, "he's been telling her it was a trick of ours."

"Well, so it was," said Mabel stoutly.

"It was indeed a wonderful trick," said Mademoiselle; "and how did you move the mannikins?"

"Oh, we've often done it—with strings, you know," Gerald explained.

"That's true, too," Kathleen whispered.

"Let us see you do once again this trick so remarkable," said Mademoiselle, arriving at the bottom-stair mat.

"Oh, I've cleared them all out," said Gerald. ("So he has," from Kathleen aside to Jimmy.) "We were so sorry you were startled; we thought you wouldn't like to see them again."

"Then," said Mademoiselle brightly, as she peeped into the untidy dining-room and saw that the figures had indeed vanished, "if we supped and discoursed of your beautiful piece of theatre?"

Gerald explained fully how much his brother and

sister would enjoy this. As for him—Mademoiselle would see that it was his duty to escort Mabel home, and kind as it was of Mademoiselle to ask her to stay the night, it could not be, on account of the frenzied and anxious affection of Mabel's aunt. And it was useless to suggest that Eliza should see Mabel home, because Eliza was nervous at night unless accompanied by her gentleman friend.

So Mabel was hatted with her own hat and cloaked with a cloak that was not hers; and she and Gerald went out by the front door, amid kind last words and appointments for the morrow.

The moment that front door was shut Gerald caught Mabel by the arm and led her briskly to the corner of the side street which led to the yard. Just round the corner he stopped.

"Now," he said, "what I want to know is—are you an idiot or aren't you?"

"Idiot yourself!" said Mabel, but mechanically, for she saw that he was in earnest.

"Because *I'm* not frightened of the Ugly-Wuglies. They're as harmless as tame rabbits. But an idiot might be frightened, and give the whole show away. If you're an idiot, say so, and I'll go back and tell them you're afraid to walk home, and that I'll go and let your aunt know you're stopping."

"I'm not an idiot," said Mabel; "and," she added, glaring round her with the wild gaze of the truly terror-stricken, "I'm not afraid of *anything*."

"I'm going to let you share my difficulties and dangers," said Gerald; "at least, I'm inclined to let you. I wouldn't do as much for my own brother, I can tell

117

you. And if you queer my pitch I'll never speak to you again or let the others either."

"You're a beast, that's what you are! I don't need to be threatened to make me brave. I *am*."

"Mabel," said Gerald, in low, thrilling tones, for he saw that the time had come to sound another note, "I *know* you're brave. I *believe* in you. That's why I've arranged it like this. I'm certain you've got the heart of a lion under that black-and-white exterior. Can I trust you? To the death?"

Mabel felt that to say anything but "Yes" was to throw away a priceless reputation for courage. So "Yes" was what she said.

"Then wait here. You're close to the lamp. And when you see me coming with *them* remember they're as harmless as serpents—I mean doves. Talk to them just like you would to any one else. See?"

He turned to leave her, but stopped at her natural question:

"What hotel did you say you were going to take them to?"

"Oh, Jimminy!" the harassed Gerald caught at his hair with both hands. "There! you see, Mabel, you're a help already"; he had, even at that moment, some tact left. "I clean forgot! I meant to ask you—isn't there any lodge or anything in the Castle grounds where I could put them for the night? The charm will break, you know, some time, like being invisible did, and they'll just be a pack of coats and things that we can easily carry home any day. Is there a lodge or anything?"

"There's a secret passage," Mabel began—but at that

118

moment the yard-door opened and an Ugly-Wugly put out its head and looked anxiously down the street.

"Righto!"—Gerald ran to meet it. It was all Mabel could do not to run in an opposite direction with an opposite motive. It was all she could do, but she did it, and was proud of herself as long as ever she remembered that night.

And now, with all the silent precaution necessitated by the near presence of an extremely insane uncle, the Ugly-Wuglies, a grisly band, trooped out of the yard-door.

"Walk on your toes, dear," the bonneted Ugly-Wugly whispered to the one with a wreath; and even at that thrilling crisis Gerald wondered how she could, since the toes of one foot were but the end of a golf club and of the other the end of a hockey-stick.

Mabel felt that there was no shame in retreating to the lamp-post at the street corner, but, once there, she made herself halt—and no one but Mabel will ever know how much making that took. Think of it—to stand there, firm and quiet, and wait for those hollow, unbelievable things to come up to her, clattering on the pavement with their stumpy feet or borne along noiselessly, as in the case of the flower-hatted lady, by a skirt that touched the ground, and had, Mabel knew very well, nothing at all inside it.

She stood very still; the insides of her hands grew cold and damp, but still she stood, saying over and over again: "They're not true—they can't be true. It's only a dream—they aren't really true. They can't be." And then Gerald was there, and all the Ugly-Wuglies crowding round, and Gerald saying:—

119

"This is one of our friends, Mabel—the Princess in the play, you know. Be a man!" he added in a whisper for her ear alone.

Mabel, all her nerves stretched tight as banjo strings, had an awful instant of not knowing whether she would be able to be a man or whether she would be merely a shrieking and running little mad girl. For the respectable Ugly-Wugly shook her limply by the hand ("He *can't* be true," she told herself), and the rose-wreathed one took her arm with a soft-padded glove at the end of an umbrella arm, and said:—

"You dear, clever little thing! *Do* walk with me!" in a gushing, girlish way, and in speech almost wholly lacking in consonants.

Then they all walked up the High Street as if, as Gerald said, they were anybody else.

It was a strange procession, but Liddlesby goes early to bed, and the Liddlesby police, in common with those of most other places, wear boots that one can hear a mile off. If such boots had been heard, Gerald would have had time to turn back and head them off. He felt now that he could not resist a flush of pride in Mabel's courage as he heard her polite rejoinders to the still more polite remarks of the amiable Ugly-Wuglies. He did not know how near she was to the scream that would throw away the whole thing and bring the police and the residents out to the ruin of everybody.

They met no one, except one man, who murmured, "Guy Fawkes, swelp me!" and crossed the road hurriedly; and when, next day, he told what he had seen, his wife disbelieved him, and also said it was a judgment on him, which was unreasonable.

Mabel felt as though she were taking part in a very completely arranged nightmare, but Gerald was in it too, Gerald, who had asked if she was an idiot. Well, she wasn't. But she soon would be, she felt. Yet she went on answering the courteous vowel-talk of these impossible people. She had often heard her aunt speak of impossible people. Well, now she knew what they were like.

Summer twilight had melted into summer moonlight. The shadows of the Ugly-Wuglies on the white road were much more horrible than their more solid selves. Mabel wished it had been a dark night, and then corrected the wish with a hasty shudder.

Gerald, submitting to a searching interrogatory from the tall-hatted Ugly-Wugly as to his schools, his sports, pastimes, and ambitions, wondered how long the spell would last. The ring seemed to work in sevens. Would these things have seven hours' life—or fourteen—or twenty-one? His mind lost itself in the intricacies of the seven-times table and only found itself with a shock when the procession found *itself* at the gates of the Castle grounds.

Locked—of course.

"You see," he explained, as the Ugly-Wuglies vainly shook the iron gates with incredible hands; "it's so very late. There *is* another way. But you have to climb through a hole."

"The ladies," the respectable Ugly-Wugly began objecting; but the ladies with one voice affirmed that they loved adventures. "So frightfully thrilling," added the one who wore roses.

So they went round by the road, and coming to the

hole—it was a little difficult to find in the moonlight, which always disguises the most familiar things—Gerald went first with the bicycle lantern which he had snatched as his pilgrims came out of the yard; the shrinking Mabel followed, and then the Ugly-Wuglies, with hollow rattlings of their wooden limbs against the stone, crept through, and with strange vowel-sounds of general amazement, manly courage, and feminine nervousness, followed the light along the passage through the fern-hung cutting and under the arch.

When they emerged on the moonlit enchantment of the Italian garden a quite intelligible "Oh!" of surprised admiration broke from more than one painted paper lip; and the respectable Ugly-Wugly was understood to say that it must be quite a show-place—by George, sir! yes.

Those marble terraces and artfully serpentining gravel walks surely never had echoed to steps so strange. No shadows so wildly unbelievable had, for all its enchantments, ever fallen on those smooth, gray, dewy lawns.

"This seems a very superior hotel," the tall-hatted Ugly-Wugly was saying; "the grounds are laid out with what you might call taste."

"We should have to go in by the back door," said Mabel suddenly. "The front door's locked at half-past nine."

A short, stout Ugly-Wugly in a yellow and blue cricket cap, who had hardly spoken, muttered something about an escapade, and about feeling quite young again.

They hastened up the steps of the Temple of Flora.

The back of it, where no elegant arch opened to the air, was against one of those sheer hills, almost cliffs, that diversified the landscape of that garden. Mabel passed behind the statue of the goddess, fumbled a little, and then Gerald's lantern, flashing like a search-light, showed a very high and very narrow doorway: the stone that was the door, and that had closed it, revolved slowly under the touch of Mabel's fingers.

"This way," she said, and panted a little. The back of her neck felt cold and goose-fleshy.

"You lead the way, my lad, with the lantern," said the suburban Ugly-Wugly in his bluff, agreeable way.

"I—I must stay behind to close the door," said Gerald.

"The Princess can do that. *We'll* help her," said the wreathed one with effusion; and Gerald thought her horribly officious.

He insisted gently that he would be the one responsible for the safe shutting of that door.

"You wouldn't like me to get into trouble, I'm sure," he urged; and the Ugly-Wuglies, for the last time kind and reasonable, agreed that this, of all things, they would most deplore.

"*You* take it," Gerald urged, pressing the bicycle lamp on the elderly Ugly-Wugly; "you're the natural leader. Go straight ahead. Are there any steps?" he asked Mabel in a whisper.

"Not for ever so long," she whispered back. "It goes on for ages, and then twists round."

"Whispering," said the smallest Ugly-Wugly suddenly, "ain't manners."

"*He* hasn't any, anyhow," whispered the lady Ugly-

123

Wugly; "don't mind him—quite a self-made man," and squeezed Mabel's arm with horrible confidential flabbiness.

The respectable Ugly-Wugly leading with the lamp, the others following trustfully, one and all disappeared into that narrow doorway; and Gerald and Mabel standing outside, hardly daring to breathe lest a breath should retard the procession, almost sobbed with relief. Prematurely, as it turned out. For suddenly there was a rush and a scuffle inside the passage, and as they strove to close the door the Ugly-Wuglies fiercely pressed to open it again. Whether they saw something in the dark passage that alarmed them, whether they took it into their empty heads that this could not be the back way to any really respectable hotel, or whether a convincing sudden instinct warned them that they were being tricked, Mabel and Gerald never knew. But they knew that the Ugly-Wuglies were no longer friendly and commonplace, that a fierce change had come over them. Cries of "No, No!" "We won't go on!" "Make *him* lead!" broke the dreamy stillness of the perfect night. There were screams from ladies' voices, the hoarse, determined shouts of strong Ugly-Wuglies roused to resistance, and, worse than all, the steady pushing open of that narrow stone door that had almost closed upon the ghastly crew. Through the chink of it they could be seen, a writhing black crowd against the light of the bicycle lamp; a padded hand reached round the door; stick-boned arms stretched out angrily towards the world that that door, if it closed, would shut them off from for ever. And the tone of their consonantless speech was no longer conciliatory and ordinary; it was threatening, full of the menace of unbearable horrors.

The padded hand fell on Gerald's arm, and instantly all the terrors that he had, so far, only known in imagination became real to him, and he saw, in the sort of flash that shows drowning people their past lives, what it was that he had asked of Mabel, and that she had given.

"Push, push for your life!" he cried, and setting his heel against the pedestal of Flora, pushed manfully.

"I can't any more—oh, I can't!" moaned Mabel, and tried to use her heel likewise, but her legs were too short.

"They mustn't get out, they mustn't!" Gerald panted.

"You'll know it when we do," came from inside the door in tones which fury and mouth-rooflessness would have made unintelligible to any ears but those sharpened by the wild fear of that unspeakable moment.

"What's up, there?" cried suddenly a new voice—a voice with all its consonants comforting, clean-cut, and ringing, and abruptly a new shadow fell on the marble floor of Flora's temple.

"Come and help push!" Gerald's voice only just reached the newcomer. "If they get out they'll kill us all."

A strong, velveteen-covered shoulder pushed suddenly between the shoulders of Gerald and Mabel; a stout man's heel sought the aid of the goddess's pedestal; the heavy, narrow door yielded slowly, it closed, its spring clicked, and the furious, surging threatening mass of Ugly-Wuglies was shut in, and Gerald and Mabel—oh, incredible relief!—were shut out. Mabel threw herself on the marble floor, sobbing slow, heavy sobs of achievement and exhaustion.

The newcomer—he appeared to be a game-keeper, Gerald decided later—looked down on—well, certainly on Mabel, and said:

"Come on, don't be a little duffer." (He may have said, "a couple of little duffers.") "Who is it, and what's it all about?"

"I can't possibly tell you," Gerald panted.

"We shall have to see about that shan't we," said the newcomer amiably. "Come out into the moonlight and let's review the situation."

What Gerald told the 'game-keeper', what became of the Ugly-Wuglies and what the magic ring ultimately did for everybody concerned, can be discovered in Edith Nesbit's story from which this extract is taken, THE ENCHANTED CASTLE, *published by Ernest Benn Ltd.*

ACKNOWLEDGEMENTS

The editor gratefully acknowledges permission to reprint copyright material to the following:

Sorche Nic Leodhas and The Bodley Head for *The Ghost that didn't want to be a Ghost* and *The Man Who Walked Widdershins Round the Kirk*.

Mrs. Croft Dickinson and Wm. Collins Ltd. for *The Keepers of the Wall* and *His Own Number*.

Ruth Sawyer and the Viking Press Inc. for *Fiddler, Play Fast, Play Faster* (© 1941).

The Executors of the estate of H. G. Wells for *The Magic Shop* and *The Flowering of the Strange Orchid*.

The Executors of the estate of Edith Nesbit, and Ernest Benn Ltd. for the extract from *The Enchanted Castle, The Ugly-Wuglies*.

ARMADA BOOKS